He'd always felt too much for her, and the past two days, those feelings had grown tenfold.

The threat of something going wrong, her getting hurt, something happening to the baby… all of it was hard to take. And the hardest thing to accept was that he had so little control of what happened next.

"What is it?" Sarah leaned forward, concern on her face.

He forced himself to take a deep breath. "Nothing. I just…" But he couldn't finish the thought. So instead, he said, "We'll find answers, Sarah. I promise."

"That's a promise you might not be able to keep."

He fitted his hands over hers and gave them a gentle squeeze. She was strong. But even strong people had vulnerabilities. Even strong people needed to be able to rely on someone.

Now that Sarah was in danger, now that they had a baby on the way, he no longer had the right to opt out. Scared, confused…none of that mattered. He had to be that someone for Sarah to rely on. And he couldn't let anything get in the way.

ANN VOSS PETERSON

ROCKY MOUNTAIN FUGITIVE

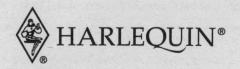

TORONTO • NEW YORK • LONDON
AMSTERDAM • PARIS • SYDNEY • HAMBURG
STOCKHOLM • ATHENS • TOKYO • MILAN • MADRID
PRAGUE • WARSAW • BUDAPEST • AUCKLAND

To Michael Voss and Ty McBride. Thanks for
showing me a whole different side of Wyoming!

Recycling programs
for this product may
not exist in your area.

ISBN-13: 978-0-373-74523-4

ROCKY MOUNTAIN FUGITIVE

Copyright © 2010 by Ann Voss Peterson

ABOUT THE AUTHOR

Ever since she was a little girl making her own books out of construction paper, Ann Voss Peterson wanted to write. So when it came time to choose a major at the University of Wisconsin, creative writing was her only choice. Of course, writing wasn't a *practical* choice—one needs to earn a living. So Ann found jobs ranging from proofreading legal transcripts, to working with quarter horses, to washing windows. But no matter how she earned her paycheck, she continued to write the type of stories that captured her heart and imagination—romantic suspense. Ann lives near Madison, Wisconsin, with her husband, her two young sons, her border collie and her quarter horse mare. Ann loves to hear from readers. E-mail her at ann@annvosspeterson.com or visit her Web site at www.annvosspeterson.com.

Books by Ann Voss Peterson

CAST OF CHARACTERS

Eric Lander—Framed for a murder he witnessed, Eric is a marked man. But he can't go on the run without first protecting the woman he can't help but love.

Sarah Trask—She's always tried to take care of her brother, but dying as a result of his schemes is too much to ask. The only man she can turn to for help is the man she loved and lost…the man who doesn't know she's carrying his child.

Randy Trask—Sarah's brother is always looking to make an easy buck. So what trouble did he get into this time?

Bracco—He told Randy a dangerous secret, and now he's dead.

Sheriff Danny Gillette—The sheriff is all about justice, even when he has to dispense it himself.

Layton Adams—He became a father figure to Sarah when his own daughter was brutally murdered. He will protect her at all costs. And as far as he sees it, she needs protection from the likes of Eric Lander.

Casey Sherwood—The eager young ranch hand has a vigilante streak. Has the sheriff convinced him to help with a scheme outside the law?

Glenn Freemont—The beleaguered ranch hand is covering for Casey. But is he helping the sheriff, too?

Walter Burne—The drug dealer wants his money and will wipe out anything and anyone in his way.

Dennis Prohaska—The jaded reporter wants to write true crime. Could Eric and Sarah be his big break?

Chapter One

No one was supposed to be up this high in the mountains. Not in the first week of June, too early in the tourist season for most recreational climbers. Not with a cold wind ushering in dark clouds from the northwest.

Hands steady on the belaying rope, Eric Lander dared a glance away from his climbing partner, Randy Trask, ten feet below him, and focused beyond the lodgepole pine stabbing the open Wyoming sky. Sure enough, the stirring of movement he'd seen in his peripheral vision was accurate. Two men. Heading their way. At this point, they were not much bigger than dots against the sparse grass and sagebrush of the slope below. But he recognized the trademark brown coats of the county sheriff's department.

"Ready to climb," Randy called.

Eric bit back his nearly automatic response.

He wasn't ready for Randy to start his climb. Not yet. There was something wrong here, something he could sense riding the wind as clear as the coming storm. And as a wilderness guide, he'd learned to listen to his instincts. "Friends of yours?"

Randy secured his hold, then squinted over the tops of the trees. His eyes flared wide. The reaction took only a split second, like the shifting of light caused by cloud wisps blowing past the sun. But the tension riding on the air increased threefold.

In light of Randy's recent history, Eric could guess the reason. "Are you in some kind of trouble?"

"It's not like that."

"Then what is it like?"

"It's just something a guy told me about."

"Let me guess. Your cell mate?"

Randy glanced away and shifted his feet on the rock shelf.

Eric had taken Randy climbing before Eric's wilderness guide business started its season with the hope of helping his old friend start a new life. He should have known better. "Damn it, Randy. You promised your sister you'd stay clean." As angry as he was with Randy, he couldn't bring himself to say Sarah's name out loud. He couldn't afford to think too much about her, either.

"I haven't done anything."

"Then why are they here?"

"I'll tell you about it later. After we get to the top of this rock face. Ready to climb."

Eric glanced back to the men. They were closer now. And they were definitely sheriff's deputies. One pointed up at them. The other was carrying a rifle.

Eric shook his head. "I don't like the look of this. We'd better rappel down."

"I can't do that."

"Then I will. See what's going on."

"You can't, either. We need to get out of here. Now." Something trembled behind Randy's words.

Something that made the back of Eric's neck prickle. "What's going on, Randy? What have you gotten us into?"

Randy blew a stream of air through tight lips. "Listen, I'm sorry. I'm into a guy for a lot of money. I thought this might be my chance to wipe the slate clean."

"What are you talking about?"

"An opportunity."

"An opportunity that you heard about from your cell mate?"

"It sounded easy. I didn't believe Bracco when he said the sheriff would be watching me. That they'd know as soon as I made a move. It seemed like something from a movie. Or one of his paranoid delusions."

Eric shook his head. Delusions? Sounded like Randy was having some delusions of his own. If they were higher on the mountain, he might be able to pass the whole thing off as altitude sickness. Yet as much as Eric wanted to explain away the deputies' presence and his old friend's fear, he couldn't shrug off the pressure assaulting the back of his neck. He needed to get control of this situation. "Rappel down to the slope, and we'll circle through the crevasse." He had to be crazy, suggesting they run away from lawmen. But the deputies hadn't made contact yet. And he needed to buy some time, figure out what was going on. As soon as he could compile a few facts, he'd lead Randy into the sheriff's department himself.

"No. We need to keep going up to Saddle Horn Ridge."

"Why?"

"Bracco said there was something big at the

campsite up there. I don't know what. I just wanted to check it out. An easy trip. Just in case he was telling the truth, you know?"

Because he owed someone money. No doubt resulting from the failure of some other "get rich quick and easy" arrangement like this one. "This isn't looking quite so easy."

"Like I said, I didn't believe his rambling about the sheriff making whoever knew about it into a marked man or whatever."

Marked man? Eric glanced down at the deputies. They were close to the rock face, now, nothing separating them but a couple of tooth-pick-straight pines and fifty feet of vertical rock. "So that's what this climb is about? We're on some sort of damned treasure hunt? A treasure hunt for something *obviously* illegal?"

"I guess."

I guess? As if he had no role in them being here? As if he hadn't begged Eric to guide him to the ridge? As if he hadn't lied? Again?

There were plenty of times Eric wanted to wring Randy's neck. So many that he'd learned to keep his distance from his old climbing buddy in the months leading up to his fraud arrest and subsequent stint in jail. But Randy had promised to turn over a new leaf, and Eric had wanted to believe him. For his friends' sake…and for Sarah's. "I can't believe you would—"

The crack of gunfire split the air.

Randy slammed into the rock as if shoved. His eyes widened, staring at Eric.

"Randy!"

"Get to the top." Randy flattened his body to the rock. A spot bloomed on his T-shirt, darker than the black cotton.

Eric didn't know what he was seeing, what he had seen. These were lawmen. They hadn't identified themselves. They hadn't said a single word. They'd just opened fire. This couldn't be happening. "Are you hit?" The words left his lips before he knew he'd spoken them. He didn't have to ask. He knew the answer.

Randy gritted his teeth. He leaned chest to rock, the fingers of one hand gripping a handhold, the other wrapped around his middle, as if trying to stop the spreading stain. "Get out of here. Go to the top. Find…"

Eric shook his head. He couldn't care less about some stolen money or drugs or whatever the hell was up there. He should have climbed down to the shelf Randy was on as soon as they saw the men. At least then he'd have a shot at reaching him, helping him. Now that Randy was hit, he didn't dare loose his grip on the belay. "Move toward me. Behind the trees." At least if Randy wasn't out in the open, the deputy wouldn't have such an easy shot. Maybe then Eric could get a hold of him, help him…where?

Down below, the deputy raised the rifle to his shoulder again.

"Randy! Move! Now!" Eric's voice rasped his throat. Begging. Pleading. Thinking of nothing but helping Randy, he surged forward, but his backline anchored him to the cliff. He couldn't breathe. His hands were sweaty, shaking. He took up all slack on the rope, resisting the urge to pull Randy to him. All that would do was knock him off balance, then they would really be in trouble. "Come on, man. You can do it. I got you on belay."

Randy shook his head and remained rooted to his spot. He made a noise deep in his throat, something between a growl and a sob. "Didn't mean for this…really, Eric…didn't believe…"

A second rifle shot shattered the air.

Randy's body jolted stiffly. He slung back in his climbing harness and sagged off the shelf's edge.

The rope yanked hard against the belay device. Eric locked it off and braced himself against the pull of his friend's weight. This couldn't be happening. "God, no. Randy."

His friend dangled ten feet below. His full weight bore down on the rope, the belaying device and Eric's break hand all that was between Randy and a fifty-foot fall onto scree at the bottom of the slope.

At least Randy was now behind the treetops. The deputy no longer had an open shot. Not that it mattered, if Randy was already dead.

Another crack split the air. Rock exploded. Something hit the crown of his head with the force of a hard kick.

He staggered, trying to lean toward rock and not plunge off the narrow shelf. His head whirled. His ears rang. Had he been hit?

He raised his hand to his head. Blood soaked his hair and dripped down his neck, hot and sticky. A scrape, not a hole. He'd only gotten nicked, probably by a chunk of rock. He'd survive.

Randy might not be so lucky.

He had to reach his friend. He had to get him out of here. Off the mountain, to town, to a hospital.

But how?

He would have to figure that out later. First he had to reach Randy. He tied off the belay rope and released his backline with shaking fingers.

In his peripheral vision, he saw the second

deputy raise his pistol. If he stayed here another second, he'd be no help to Randy or himself. He'd be dead.

Praying his anchor in the rock would hold under their weight, he grabbed the rope and stepped off the ledge.

The pistol cracked below.

Eric braced himself for the cut of the bullet. It missed, pinging off the rock face above. He lowered himself down the rope, palms sweaty on nylon.

When he reached Randy, he knew his friend was already dead. He could feel it, sense it. Securing a hold on the rock, he checked Randy's pulse to be sure. His skin was warm, but no throb beat against Eric's touch. He checked the other side of his throat, moving his fingers several times. Praying he'd detect something. Anything. But he felt nothing at all.

Shouts rose from the men below.

Eric's breath shuddered deep in his chest. He couldn't help Randy. Not anymore. Now he could only help himself. He had to think. He had to get out of here or he would share the same fate as his friend.

A marked man.

The words blared in the back of Eric's mind.

By trying to find whatever it was up on Saddle Horn Ridge, had Randy marked himself for death? Had he marked everyone he was close to? Eric? Layton, the foreman at the ranch?

Sarah?

Eric scanned the rock face. He had to get out of here, like Randy said, but he wasn't climbing to Saddle Horn Ridge. He had to get to the ranch. He had to make sure Sarah was all right.

And he had to do it now.

Chapter Two

Sarah was leaning down from her gelding's back to lock the yearlings in the corral when Radar started barking. Straightening in the saddle, she focused on the SUV pulling up the long gravel drive. It swung past the house and headed for the barn, finally coming to a stop on the other side of the fence. A lone man dismounted from the vehicle and strode toward her.

The brim of his silver belly hat shaded his eyes, but Sarah had no trouble recognizing Sheriff Danny Gillette. The last time she'd seen him was months before, at her brother's trial. He was bald as a baby pig under that cowboy hat, and his voice held the growl of a man who'd smoked his way through life. She could still recite his brutal condemnation of her brother.

"That'll do, Radar," she called to the dog. He stopped barking, but remained alert, his white-tipped tail waving like a flag in the constant basin wind.

The sheriff rested one boot on the lower rail of the fence and skimmed his gaze over corral, barns and rough pastureland beyond. The place was quiet, vacant. Her foreman, Layton, and two ranch hands had taken a herd of steers to graze land she'd leased from the Bureau of Land Management and wouldn't be back for hours. But as much as she wanted to tell herself the sheriff was here to talk to Keith or Glenn about a drunken brawl at the nearby Full Throttle saloon, she doubted that was the case.

Sarah let out a shaky breath and rolled her shoulders back, trying to loosen the cramp bearing down on the back of her neck. Not even twenty-four hours since Randy had gotten out of jail, and the sheriff was already paying a call. She sure as hell hoped he meant it only as a warning. Randy promised he'd stay clean if she let him stay at the ranch while he got his feet under him. He'd better have kept his word.

She resisted the urge to cup her hand over her middle. In her fourth month, she was just starting to show, but the urge to cover her belly every time she felt nervous or defensive had started before she'd even admitted to herself that she was pregnant. Somehow her body had known before her brain. She rubbed her palm on her thigh.

Better get this over with.

Bringing a leg to her gelding's side, she pushed him into a lope. When they reached the far side of the corral, she lifted her rein hand and brought her mount to a stop with just a touch of slide. "Can I help you, Sheriff?"

"Miss Trask," he said with a nod of his head. He pulled a package of smokes from his shirt pocket and tapped it on the heel of an upturned hand. "We need to have a little talk about your brother."

ERIC SPOTTED THE SHERIFF'S SUV as soon as he crested the hill. The half-dozen horses milling behind the corral fence kicked up dust, dulling the SUV's white gleam, but even though he was too far away to make out the sheriff department's emblem on the door, Eric knew who the vehicle belonged to.

It hadn't been easy making it down off the mountain while avoiding the armed deputies. Fortunately he knew the peaks in this area better than he knew his own heart. If he hadn't, he never would have been able to work his way into the crevasse to the north of the rock face where Randy died. He never would have been able to make his way down, past the slope where the deputies scoured the mountain through their rifle scopes. He wouldn't have been able to reach the guide cabin at the base of the mountain and retrieve his truck.

He had gotten away unseen, all right. But it had taken him too long.

He scanned the corrals and outbuildings. Sarah's pickup sat in front of the house. But other than the horses in the corral, he could see no movement. The Buckrail only employed a foreman and three hands, but every time Eric had visited, the place had been bustling. Now it looked vacant. The big stock trailer was nowhere to be seen.

Where was Sarah?

Eric forced back the urge to push the pedal to the floor and race down the remaining half mile to the ranch. Rushing in like some sort of damn knight would only get him killed, and probably Sarah, too. He had to be smart about his next move. He had to think.

He raised his hand to his throbbing head.

Pulling the truck off the dirt road, he bounced

over rough ground to a rock outcropping. He parked out of sight on the far side.

He'd regretted not taking a weapon with him on the climb with Randy. He wouldn't make that mistake this time. He twisted in his seat.

The rack in the back window of the cab was empty, the locking mechanism broken. His hunting rifle was gone.

Damn, damn, damn. He hadn't thought to look when he'd reached his truck. He'd just wanted to get out of there as quickly as possible. But he had a good idea of who had taken it. The deputies who'd shot Randy. And he had a bad feeling his rifle was the weapon they'd used.

He gripped the wheel in front of him. He couldn't think about the implications of that. Not now. The only thing he could afford to focus on was Sarah. He had to make sure she was okay.

He climbed out of the truck, strode to the back and opened the tailgate. There had to be something inside he could use for a weapon. He focused on the tire iron clamped down under the spare. It would have to do.

He released the spare and grabbed the tire iron. Testing the heft in his hand, he circled the red rock and set off in a steady run. He'd approach the house and barns from an angle, instead of straight on. He didn't have much on his side. He needed surprise.

He set off for the house first. Tufts of rough grass and sagebrush dotted the rocky soil. Still, after the mountain terrain, the short trek was easy. He reached the back of the house without seeing a soul. He didn't have to peer in the darkened windows to know no one was there. No one seemed to be anywhere. Not even the bark of her Border collie, Radar, broke the stillness.

He needed to check the barn.

Negotiating the maze of wood rail fence, he crossed corrals and circled loafing sheds until he reached the two-story barn. Flies buzzed in his ears. One landed on his forehead. He brushed it away, his hand coming back sticky with drying blood. At least the gush had slowed, but pain still throbbed through his skull.

Pushing the pain away, he wiped his hand on his jeans, climbed the fence and dropped into the corral closest to the barn.

There were few horses in the corrals, and most looked too young to work cattle. Three of the horses gathered around him, nickering and nudging him with their noses. Others pawed the ground and chased one another, jockeying for the best positions in front of the feeders.

The sun was already hovering just above the peaks to the west, its feeble glow quickly being overtaken by the leading edge of storm clouds. Sarah was adamant about her livestock being fed on time. She was never late.

Dust rose into the air thick as fog and whirled in the wind. In front of the barn door, Eric caught a glimpse of black-and-white fur.

Sarah's dog wouldn't be far from his mistress. She had to be in the barn. But the fact that Radar wasn't inside with her had him worried.

He raced across the corral, horses swirling around him. He couldn't afford to think too hard about what might have already happened to Sarah. He had to stay alert. He was used to testing himself against rock, snow and rough mountain terrain, not a living adversary. Certainly not armed lawmen. He needed to be ready.

Radar spun away from the door and stared at him, one ear pricked.

Eric froze. He knew the dog, but he hadn't been around for months now. The last thing he needed was for Radar to start barking, tipping off whomever was inside.

Eric raised a hand. Tilting his palm downward, he lowered his hand, gesturing for the dog to lie down the way he'd seen Sarah do countless times.

Radar crouched to the ground. Still watching, he stayed silent.

Blowing a breath through tense lips, Eric scaled the final fence and crept to the barn. The center part of the structure rose to two stories. Each side only contained one, the roofs slanting over stall areas. He stepped to the center door. The deep hum of a male voice came from inside. An inch of space gaped between the sliding door's two halves. The barn was dark inside. If Eric stood directly in front of the door, or even peered inside, he would block the feeble light. From inside, his presence would be as obvious as if he'd rang a damn doorbell.

He tried to hear over the loud beat of his pulse.

"Where was he headed?"

Eric recognized the low, graveled voice of the sheriff himself.

"What was your brother looking for?"

"I don't know. He went climbing. That's all he told me."

A jumble of emotion spun through Eric's mind and settled like an ache in his chest. He'd tried to drive Sarah's strong contralto from his memory. He hadn't succeeded. But hearing it again, under these circumstances…

it was all he could do to keep from throwing the barn door open and rushing in to protect her.

In light of the way things had ended between them, she'd probably find that ironic.

"Who has your brother talked to since he was released?"

"I don't know. No one, I guess. He's only got home last night. Did he do something? What is this about?"

"I'm not messing around here, Miss Trask. Eric Lander. You. Who else?"

"I want to talk to a lawyer. I have the right to see a lawyer."

"Listen," the sheriff said, his voice getting quiet, controlled in a way that made Eric's pulse spike. "You have the right to tell me what I want to know, or I'll have to assume you're in this as deep as your brother."

Eric stepped away from the door. He couldn't stand here and listen any longer. He'd been slow to act to help Randy. Slow to figure out what kind of danger the two of them were in. Slow to believe the deputies were not there to uphold the law. He wasn't going to make the same mistake again. He needed to find a way inside. He needed some kind of strategy. Some way to take control of the situation before the sheriff could draw his gun. Before he could hurt Sarah.

Think.

He knew the barn's layout. Hell, he'd helped Sarah feed enough times in their few months together that he should be able to move around the ranch in the dark.

Think.

He pictured the inside of the barn in his mind's eye. The place was small, only a half-dozen stalls, a wash stall and a good sized tack-and-feed room. Judging from the closeness of the sheriff's voice, he and Sarah were in the main barn area, not closed off in the tack room. That meant Eric should be able to see them from one of the windows above.

As long as he could get up on the roof without giving himself away.

He circled to the flank of the barn, climbing over fences and dodging demanding horses. Reaching a spot where the roof slanted low, in back of the barn, he focused on the windows used to let natural light into the structure and shoved the tire iron in the back waistband of his jeans. The metal was cold against his skin. Bracing. Its chill sharpened his focus and resolve. He eyed the wood siding. Freshly painted a rich brown, it held few spots to get finger holds, let alone a spot for a toe.

Good thing Eric didn't need much.

Fitting his fingers into the ridges between the planks, he pulled himself up the siding and grasped the edge of the roof. He pulled himself onto the shingles and scrambled up to the windows under the upper eaves. The windows were locked. Holding his breath, he jimmied the pane up and down and prayed the sheriff wouldn't hear. The lock popped open. He slid the glass wide and listened for movement from inside the barn.

Below in the corral, horses snorted and whinnied. A cloud of dust plumed on the crest of the hill. Another vehicle heading this way... another sheriff's department SUV.

A wave of dizziness swept over him. Clamping down on the inside of his lower lip, he concentrated on opening the door without losing his balance. He couldn't let himself think about all the things that could go wrong. If he wanted to get Sarah out of this mess, he had to focus.

He pushed his head through the open window and looked down into the barn aisle. The scent of wood shavings and manure stuck thick in his throat and tickled his nose.

"Horse accidents are funny things," the sheriff's voice boomed from below. "They can happen at any time. To anyone. Even people who work with horses every day."

"I can't come up with answers I don't have."

Sarah's voice sounded forceful, but there was a sharp tinge to it Eric knew came from fear. He leaned farther into the barn to get a better angle.

The sheriff stood almost directly below. He reached up to a peg holding a collection of old horseshoes. He grasped one and shook it up and down as if testing its heft. "Something unexpected can happen, spook the horse, and…"

Sarah pressed against the wall of the wash stall. She was a slender woman, all sinew and muscle developed by back-breaking ranch work. But the woman he was looking at was softer than he remembered. More vulnerable. Her hands were behind her back, and when she moved, Eric could see a set of handcuffs bound her to a metal rail.

"No threat. I'm stating fact." Sheriff Gillette slapped the steel shoe against his palm.

Eric didn't know what he'd missed while climbing to the loft, but he sure as hell wasn't going to let this go any further. He pulled the tire iron from the back of his jeans.

The sheriff looked up. He reached for his gun.

Chapter Three

Sarah leaned back on the wash stall wall and lashed out with a foot. She connected with the sheriff's ankle, the force shuddering through her boot and up her leg.

A shot exploded in her ears.

A body landed on the sheriff, knocking him to the ground. A body…oh, God…Eric.

For a moment, she couldn't think. She couldn't breathe.

Eric shoved a forearm under the sheriff's jaw, bending his head back. He grabbed the sheriff's gun hand and slammed it against the floor. The gun skittered across the ground. He picked it up, and held it on the sheriff. The side of his face was covered with dried blood. "Get up."

Sarah's legs wobbled, weak with relief.

The sheriff struggled to a sitting position, holding his hand to the side of his head. His hat lay in the dust several feet away. "You don't want to do this, son."

"No. You're right. I want to just kill you and take the handcuff key off your dead body. Unless that's what you want, too, you'd better get the hell up."

The sheriff struggled to his feet. "What you're doing here is against the law."

"Oh, you mean like gunning down a man in cold blood? Or preparing to beat on a shackled woman with a damn horseshoe? Those kinds of against the law?"

The sheriff squinted. "You're Lander."

"Keys," Eric ordered.

Gillette pulled a key ring from his pocket, and Eric snatched it from his fingers.

Eric unlocked one of Sarah's wrists and handed her the keys. Once she freed herself, he motioned to the sheriff. She slipped the shackles around one fat wrist and slipped the cuff around the steel bars of a nearby stall before securing his second.

She rubbed her sore arms. She couldn't make sense of any of this. First the sheriff. Now Eric's sudden appearance. He was supposed to be climbing with Randy.

Barking erupted outside.

Sarah's mind raced. Someone was here. Layton? Keith and Glenn?

The sheriff glanced over his shoulder and smirked. "Looks like my backup is here. Sure you don't want to rethink this?"

"Backup?"

"That's right. You might as well give yourselves up right now. It'll go easier on you."

Ignoring Gillette, Eric grabbed her arm. "Hurry." He pulled her toward the barn's back door, and they slipped into the corral. Yearlings gathered around them, looking for dinner. Something raced around the side of the barn, a black-and-white streak.

"Radar."

He headed straight for her. Flying through the air the last few feet, he bounced off her thigh with his front paws and started back the other way, as if he was playing a game.

He was telling her something, that someone was here. "Radar." The dog's head snapped around at her serious tone. He bounced back to her side.

Eric pulled her through the gathering horses. "We have to get out of here."

"What is happening? Where is—"

"We'll talk later."

Men's voices rose from the front of the barn. "Who's here?"

"Deputies. And they aren't here to help."

He wasn't making sense. None of this was making any sense. She bit back the questions crowding at the tip of her tongue. "Where do we go?"

"My truck is up by the rocks, but I don't think we can get there. Not without being spotted." He spun back to the corral. "Are any of these horses broke to ride?"

She scanned the group of yearlings, stopping on the only older mare in the bunch. "She is." She led Eric to the mare, Radar following at their heels.

Grabbing a handful of mane, she raised a foot. Eric grabbed her lower leg and boosted her onto the mare's back. He swung open the gate leading to the pasture.

"Stop. They're back here."

Sarah's throat closed. At first she almost did as he said. Almost dismounted right there and gave herself up. He was a deputy, wasn't he? She was no criminal. He had to be there to help, didn't he?

Unlike the sheriff?

She didn't have to think too hard to remember the threat in the sheriff's eyes, the brutal tone in his voice, the way he lifted the horseshoe implying he'd use it on her.

"Sarah." Eric held up an arm, about to swing his leg up.

She looked down at him. Eric was no criminal, either. She was more sure of that than anything. They had to get out of here. She grabbed his arm, and he vaulted into place behind her. She laid her heel into the mare's side and they broke into a full bore gallop.

THEY'D RACED ALL THE way to the creek before Eric dared take a breath. The mare slowed as she approached the water, breaking to a jog before splashing into the shallow current. Sarah's dog plunged in behind.

"Follow the river bed," Eric said.

Sarah directed the horse upstream. Her dark hair whipped in the wind, lashing against his face. "You think they'll track us?"

"Can't be too careful." He was still shaken from the moment he looked down the barrel of the sheriff's gun, the split second before Sarah's kick made his shot go wide. "You saved my life back there."

"I have a feeling you might have saved mine, too." She turned her head to the side, letting her words drift back to him more easily. From this angle he could see the sweep of her eyelashes and the curve of her cheek through her dark cascade of hair. "Are you going to tell me what's going on?"

"I'd like to, but I don't really know myself."

"Where's Randy?"

He swallowed into a dry throat. He didn't have the words to tell her. And neither of them had the time. "We need to get moving. I'll explain things once we put more distance behind us."

"Where are we going?"

Now that was a damn good question. Obviously they couldn't call 911. "Our best bet is to get ourselves across the county line. Get out of Gillette's jurisdiction."

"This is ridiculous. All of this. This is a nightmare. There must be some kind of mistake."

"That's what I've been telling myself. Only problem is, the nightmare just keeps going, whether we take control or not. I've opted to take control."

Her chest rose and fell in a deep breath. Finally she nodded. "So we head for the county line."

The Big Horn Basin was a huge plain rimmed with mountains on all sides. County lines fell along mountain ranges and across open territory. He eyed the mountains to the west. "How long will it take if we go to the east?

"Maybe a couple of days by horse."

That sounded about right. And with a storm hovering over the mountains bringing rain and maybe even snow, it would take longer if they chose to go to the west. "Any better ideas?"

"Layton lives closer."

The thought of pulling someone else into this web Randy had tangled them in made Eric feel sick to his stomach. "I don't know…"

"He's been the Buckrail's foreman since before my parents left. He was more of a father to me than my own dad. We can trust him."

"That's not my worry."

"What is?"

He tried to swallow, but his throat wouldn't cooperate. He didn't even have to close his eyes to see the way Randy jolted when he took the first bullet. No warning. No way out.

"Eric? I need to know what's going on, and I need to know now."

He shook his head. Not now. Not until he could look her straight in the eye. Not until she had time to let the tragic news sink in. Not until she had time to cry.

A sound tickled the horizon, rising over the splash and babble of the stream. Radar froze and pricked his ears.

"Stop the horse."

"Whoa." Sarah shifted back, her hips settling against Eric's thighs. The mare stopped in the stream and lowered her head for a drink.

A growl vibrated low in Radar's chest.

Eric strained to hear over the babbling water. It took a second for the sound to register, but once it did, he knew the danger was far from over and their escape far from assured. "Bloodhounds."

Sarah tilted her head. "You're sure?"

"I wish I could say no. How the hell did they get them to the ranch so quickly?"

"What do we do?"

"Keep moving upstream, for one."

Sarah clucked, and the mare lifted her head. She broke into a trot, water splashing around them.

Eric held on to Sarah, a hand on either side of her waist. He didn't know much about scent-tracking dogs, but he'd heard they could do re-markable things. He was far from sure that a trot upstream would keep the animals from picking up their trail on the other side of the water. Not unless there was something else to draw their attention.

They continued for another mile, maybe two. The barking grew louder, clearer. One dog. Probably no more. The sound drew out into a half bark, half howl.

The animal had picked up a scent.

Sarah turned her head to the side. "Eric?"

Even though he couldn't see her expression, he could feel the alarm in her muscles, hear it in her voice. Not that he didn't have enough of his own. "We need to give the dog something else to track."

"Something else? What?"

"Will Radar go back to the ranch if you order him to?" He wasn't sure the dog would follow Radar instead of them, but it might be worth a shot.

She glanced down at the black-and-white Border collie prancing in the stream as if thrilled to be on this grand adventure. "I doubt it. He's never good about leaving me. He'd probably just double back as soon as he got out of my sight."

One idea down. He only had one more. And it wasn't his first choice by a long shot. "How far to Layton's house?"

She glanced around as if taking stock of the landscape. Though with few discernable features nearby other than hills and sagebrush, he wasn't sure what she was seeing. "Seven miles. Maybe eight."

He nodded. Not bad for country where it often took a half hour or more of driving through un-inhabited wilderness to get anywhere.

"He should be home by the time we get there."

Better if he wasn't. That way they could use his phone, borrow supplies or even a vehicle from him and yet manage not to drag him into this mess. "Do you think we can make it that far on foot?"

"Not before nightfall."

He glanced at the last glow of sun beyond the shadow of distant mountains. In this case, darkness would help them. With cloud cover and no sunlight, they might not be able to move very quickly, but neither would their pursuers.

"I can find the way after dark."

Of course she could. She had grown up on this land, and worked it every day of her life. She knew it better than he knew anything, even the mountains. "What do you think of sending the mare back to the ranch?"

"You're thinking the tracking dog will keep following her and not us?"

"Something like that."

"She's getting tired anyway. She'll probably be glad to be rid of us. And she'll be glad to be back at the barn before nightfall."

At least they had a plan, although the thought of being out in the middle of this vast open country on foot made him more than uneasy. He was used to the vertical wilderness. All this horizontal space made him feel small. And vulnerable.

He slipped off the horse's back. The water came to his knees, gurgling and swirling, cold as death. His hiking boots filled with water. His legs ached to the bone. He helped Sarah dismount.

"Okay, girl. Go back home." She smacked the horse on the rear and the mare trotted through the stream and up the bank. Once she hit dry land, she broke into a gallop and disappeared in the direction of the barn.

Sarah turned back to face Eric. Tears sparkled in her eyes and spiked her lashes, but her cheeks remained dry, as if she was fighting for composure. "I need to know what happened, Eric."

"We need to make some time. My legs are already going numb."

She started trudging upstream. "He was supposed to be climbing with you."

He opened his mouth, then closed it.

Emotion bombarded him. How on earth could he find the words?

She didn't look at him. Instead she wrapped both arms around her stomach and kept moving forward. "Please. I need to know."

"He didn't mean for anything to happen. He just…" A sob lodged in Eric's throat. He pushed it back, but if he opened his mouth again, he knew he wouldn't be able to keep the emotion in check. He could feel Sarah watching him.

"Randy's dead, isn't he?"

Somehow Eric managed to nod.

"How?" Her voice was quiet, barely a whisper, as if it had taken every ounce of strength in her to say the word.

Eric fixed his gaze on a clump of big sage about ten feet away from the creek's bank. As long as he focused on that clump and on trudging forward in the cold water, he might be able to get the words out. "He was shot in order to keep him from reaching Saddle Horn Ridge."

"By the sheriff?"

"By two deputies."

He could hear Sarah gasping for breath. She was crying. He could feel her sobs in his own chest, taking over. He could almost smell her tears. He wanted to say soothing words. To touch her. To take her in his arms. Something. But he doubted his touch would be welcome. Besides, one move toward her and he feared he'd crumble.

They kept walking. Finally she swiped at her eyes and cheeks. "Why?"

"I'm not sure."

"What do you *think* was the reason? Take a flying guess." The pitch of her voice rose. The mix of anger and fear and need ate away at him like acid.

He pulled a breath into tight lungs. He had to find a way to explain it. At least the small part he knew. He owed her that much.

Still careful not to look at her, he told her about the cell mate named Bracco. The mystery Randy was searching for at the top of Saddle Horn Ridge.

"What's up there?"

"Randy didn't know."

"But no doubt he thought it would be an easy score."

"He owes someone money."

Sarah nodded as if that was all he needed to say.

Worry over Randy had been what drew him and Sarah together in the first place. After her brother's fraud conviction, she'd needed to talk to someone who knew him, someone who cared. As an old climbing buddy who'd spent more than a few worried thoughts on Randy Trask, Eric had fit the bill. As they'd spent time together, it had ceased being about Randy. It had been strong and passionate and all-consuming. And finally it had grown to the point where it had ceased being possible. At least for Eric.

Eric shook his head. It had taken Randy's death to throw them back together again. Even worse, Randy's newest scheme had almost gotten them both killed.

And it was far from over.

He stared out at the twilight glow on the horizon and kept plunging on. He couldn't think about Randy. He couldn't think about what he and Sarah had almost had. Not now. Now he needed all his concentration. He had to focus on one thing—getting Sarah to her foreman's house, where they could call for help. Because if he couldn't do that, none of the rest mattered.

They trudged through the stream bed, water splashing to their knees, rocks slippery under their feet. Radar followed behind. The baying stopped. Shadows lengthened and darkness crept over the land. Finally Eric dared to step out on dry land. He reached out a hand to help Sarah over the rocks and tangle of vegetation.

She didn't accept his offer. Once on solid ground, she faced him. "Eric."

He willed himself to look at her. Pink rimmed her eyes. Dust and tears streaked her face. But the way she raised her chin and met his gaze made him dread what was coming next. "What?"

"I want to hire you."

He frowned. Not what he expected. Not at all. "Hire me?"

"I'm going up to Saddle Horn Ridge, and I want you to be my guide."

Chapter Four

For a moment, Eric looked like he was about to clap a hand over Sarah's mouth and demand she take back what she'd said. "Weren't you listening?"

She'd listened. And what she'd heard had her trembling more violently than she had after escaping Sheriff Gillette. But feeling shaken and scared didn't change the facts. And fear didn't erase what she needed to do. "I'm going up to Saddle Horn Ridge. I'm going to find out what this is all about."

He turned away from her and trudged over the rocky shore and through Russian olive, grass and sagebrush, grown large and thick from the nearby water source.

Sarah set off after him. Radar trotted beside, glancing from her to Eric like a child caught in the middle of his parents' argument.

Parents.

Sarah fought the urge to clutch an arm over her abdomen. She couldn't think of that right now. She had enough to deal with in the present. Enough to absorb. Right now all she could focus on was what had happened to Randy and how she and Eric could escape the same fate.

"I've climbed before. I'm in shape." She resisted the urge to look down at the slight bulge in her belly. If this had happened a month ago, she didn't know where she would have gotten the energy. The fatigue of early pregnancy had come as a shock. While she'd been ready for the nausea, that bone-deep weariness had nearly flattened her. But her stamina had started to return in the past two weeks. And although she felt drained from the ebb of adrenaline after their escape from the sheriff, she was infinitely more capable than she had been in the first three months of her pregnancy. "I do physical work every day. A little hiking and climbing isn't going to kill me."

"Hiking and climbing? I'm more concerned about flying bullets."

"The bullets are just as likely to fly if we run away as they are if we try to find out what's going on."

He looked to the side, as if absorbed in contemplating a tangle of sagebrush.

"There's something up there, Eric."

"Of course there's something. Something that got your brother killed. Something that could get you killed, too."

"Whatever it is, the sheriff already thinks I know about it. And you…you were there when Randy…" Her throat felt thick. She swallowed and blinked back the mist assaulting her eyes. Her lower lids ached, swollen from squeezing out a seemingly endless flood of tears. She still couldn't believe this was happening. That it had happened. That they were on the run from a sheriff who wanted to harm them. That her big brother had gone out on a hiking trip and now he was dead. "They know you saw everything."

"Which is why I'm not taking you to the ridge. It's too dangerous."

"But if we could find what this is all about, maybe we could use it."

"Use it for what?"

"I don't know." Right now what she wanted most was to have Randy back. And no matter what they found on that ridge, that would never be. "To stop the sheriff. To let us return to our lives."

"To make Randy's killers pay?"

"What's wrong with that?"

"Nothing. It's what I want, too. But rushing into the same situation that got your brother killed is not the way to do it."

"Then what is?"

"Getting to Layton's house. Calling for help."

"Who do we call? Not the county 911."

"There are other law enforcement agencies. We call one of them. State police. Even the FBI."

"And what if they don't believe us? We can't run for the rest of our lives."

"It's better than not having a rest of our lives."

She shook her head. She wasn't sure of that. Ranching was the only life she'd ever wanted. The open sky. The freedom she felt on the back of a horse. The strength that came with hard work and autonomy and knowing the land. She didn't even want to think of a life on the run.

And Eric. He liked to control things, be in charge. He would gladly be responsible for the world, as long as he had a say. Being on the run, always reacting, never in control…it would kill him. He would never choose that, not if he were choosing for himself. "If you were in this alone, you'd go up on that ridge. You'd find out what this is about."

He slowed his stride and glanced back at her. For the first time since she'd brought up the idea of going to the ridge, the hard line of his mouth softened. "But I'm not in this alone." His voice sounded soft, too. Tender.

She pulled her gaze away and stared out at the dark forms of rock and sagebrush, growing more sparse the farther they traveled from water. She wanted to turn back time. Go back before Randy was killed, before he'd decided to take his damn hiking trip. Before everything had gotten so terribly broken.

She knew she was being ridiculous, but she couldn't help it. Just as she couldn't stop the yearning to give in to the softness in Eric's voice. To open herself to him. To pretend trusting him to be there for her was a luxury she could afford.

She watched him out of the corner of her eye. Even in the dimming twilight, she could see the taut muscles along his jaw, the light stubble, just a shade darker than his sandy brown hair. He still looked like the same Eric, so much that even now she wanted to reach out and skim her fingers along his cheek.

She'd wondered if Eric had noticed the change in her body as they galloped bareback away from the ranch, his hands around her waist. At one time his heat pressed against her back would have reduced her to a puddle of need. This time, all she could think about was whether he felt the bulge in her tummy. The solid life growing there.

Did he suspect?

If things were different, she would have been thrilled to tell him. If they were still together. If he hadn't left.

She could still kick herself. The moment she'd uttered the damn *M* word, she'd wished she could bite it back. It had been a generic reference. Nothing about the two of them getting married. Just a fantasy of a wedding in the little basin behind the ranch house she'd had as a starry-eyed teen. But as soon as the comment had left her lips, she'd seen the look on his face.

She'd gotten too comfortable. Too trusting. She'd forgotten to be careful and had just said what was on her mind. At least he'd waited until the next day to break it off.

Radar looked up at her, searching for a way to help. Her dog would stick with her no matter what. Do what she wanted. Follow her anywhere. Men weren't quite that easy.

She swallowed into an aching throat. That

was all in the past. Dead and done. But focusing on the mistakes she'd made with Eric was easier than thinking too hard about what had happened to Randy or what the future might bring. "If you don't want to guide me up there, Eric, I can always go alone."

He wiped a hand over his face. "You could, but you won't. We'll call the state police, the attorney general, the FBI. Report all that's happened. They can take care of whatever is on that ridge *and* the sheriff at the same time."

Sarah pressed her lips together, her steps slowing, stopping. Fatigue bore down on her shoulders and made her legs heavy. A moment ago, she thought she had the energy to take on anything. Gillette. Eric. The climb to Saddle Horn Ridge. Now she wasn't so sure.

She cupped her hand over her abdomen. She had to think for more than herself. Her life wasn't the only one she was risking. And as much as she wanted to tell Eric he was wrong about what she would or wouldn't do, if there was a safer way out, she needed to take it. "Fine. We'll call."

"It's the right decision, Sarah." Eric glanced down at her arm. His brows dipped in a frown.

She let her arm fall to her side and resumed

walking. Feeling him watching her, she could only hope he was trying to figure out her change of heart and not mulling over what her protective gesture might mean.

ERIC DIDN'T HAVE TO ask if Sarah had been serious about climbing to Saddle Horn Ridge on her own. He recognized that jut of her chin, those thrown-back shoulders, that look in her eye as if she was daring anyone to get in her way. She'd do it. And he couldn't have stopped her if she hadn't changed her mind. He was both relieved and surprised she'd seen things his way.

And a little suspicious.

They trudged toward the light that marked Layton's place twinkling in the distance. The silvery sheen of sagebrush dotted the path in front of them like bumpers in an old barroom pinball game. Eric could sense wildlife around him, and prayed one of them didn't step on a rattler yet to descend into his hole for the night. He watched Radar for warning of anything his own senses didn't pick up.

But mostly he stole glances at Sarah.

He'd thought she looked different the moment he saw her in the barn. Softer. More curvy. Even now he wanted to reach out and touch her, pull her into his arms.

He shook his head. As attractive as he found her, he'd made his decision three months ago. And he knew not letting the connection between them get out of hand was the right one, even now. Sarah couldn't be part of his life, and he certainly wasn't up to being part of hers. The emotions tangling inside him were proof of that. It seemed every moment around her was a struggle to keep his head on straight. The scent of her skin. The sound of her voice. The way she made him feel alive just by glancing his way.

He brought his focus back to the mountains. This was going to be tougher than he'd thought. Not that he'd ever imagined being around Sarah and not touching her would be easy. That was precisely why he'd left after dating for only five months. If he didn't get out then, he wasn't getting out.

And he was worried about the consequences for both of them.

The wind picked up from the west and carried rain with it. The downpour was hard and short-lived, like most in the area. They kept walking through it following the light they could no longer see. By the time the storm blew over, they were soaked to the skin. The strong scent of wet sage permeated the night air.

Sarah walked with both arms wrapped tightly around her body. Her hair curled, cupping wet around cheekbones, jaw and collarbone. Her chin trembled with an endless shiver.

"You okay?" He wished he had a jacket to put around her shoulders. As it was, he was starting to shiver, too.

"Fine."

He doubted that. But at least he could get her to Layton's. The foreman would take care of her. Get her clothes dry. Lend them a phone. It would all be over soon.

Layton's place was less than impressive. A small trailer nestled at the foot of a flat-topped hill referred to as a bench. At least the bench offered some shelter from the wicked basin winds. To the rear of the trailer sat a nice-sized horse barn flanked on one side by a corral fenced in lodgepole pine rails. As far as Eric knew, Layton's horses were kept at the Buckrail. But all horse people he'd ever met invested far more in their horse operation than their own homes. Layton Adams seemed to fit that mold to a *T.*

"Looks like no one's home."

Earlier he'd been surprised Layton wasn't at the ranch. If the foreman and the other hands had been, the sheriff would never have been able to nearly get away with hurting Sarah. "Where is he?"

"He and the other hands took a herd of steers to the BLM. I knew they'd be late getting back, but he should have been home by now."

Eric nodded. The BLM was a shorthand way of describing the vast amount of acreage in Wyoming controlled by the federal government's Bureau of Land Management. Sarah must have leased some of the land to graze her cattle. "Maybe he got detained."

Sarah snapped around to stare at him. "You think the sheriff might do something to Layton?"

"I'm sure he's okay." Truth was, he didn't know. And judging from the way Sarah looked at him, she took his assurances for what they were worth. Not much.

He gestured to the trailer. "Is there any way we can get in? Use his phone?"

"I don't have a key, if that's what you mean. And I doubt he would stash one outside. Not after what happened to his daughter. He's been pretty paranoid about things like locking doors ever since."

"His daughter?" As long as Eric had known Layton, he was a man alone. No wife. No family. He lived for his work and the only emotional attachment he seemed to have to anyone was his devotion to Sarah. "I didn't know Layton had a family."

"His daughter was murdered."

"Murdered?"

"It happened years ago. Layton's daughter was shot at a friend's slumber party. An ex-boyfriend of one of the girls. It was the stuff of legends at my school. Only difference was, I knew one of the families."

"Man. That had to be tough."

"He and his wife split a few months later. That's when he came to work at the Buckrail."

Eric wiped a hand over his face. It explained a lot about Layton. The man had no sense of humor and little personality. Life had obviously kicked it out of him.

But as bad as he felt for the Buckrail's foreman, all the sympathy in the world didn't earn them the use of a phone. "Is there some other way in?"

"You mean break in?"

"You got a better idea?"

Sarah frowned at the tiny trailer. "If you lift me up to a window, maybe I can jimmy the lock."

They wound through Layton's sorry excuse for a lawn, shadows making the sage look as big as hedges. When they reached the trailer, Eric clasped his hands and lowered them, ready to boost Sarah up to the window like he'd boosted her onto the bay mare's back.

A click and scrape came from somewhere behind his head. The sound of a rifle chambering a round. "What the hell do you think you're doing?"

Chapter Five

"Layton." Sarah turned and wobbled on one foot, her other cradled in Eric's hands. "It's okay, Layton. It's me."

She could barely see her foreman's frown in the darkness. He held a long gun at the ready, its barrel pointing square in the center of Eric's back. At her feet, Radar scootched in close, trying to catch Layton's attention. His wagging tail wiggled his whole body.

"Sarah." Layton glanced at her but didn't lower the weapon. "Thank God you're okay."

"I'm glad you're here. Some bad things are happening. We need to use your phone."

Layton's bushy gray brows dipped. His narrowed eyes drilled into Eric's back. "Bad things. Yeah, I heard."

Eric released her foot. He started to straighten. "Don't move, son."

Sarah stepped toward him. "Layton—"

"Careful, Sarah. I don't think you know what this man here has done."

"Done?" She scrambled to make sense of what he was saying. Eric had done nothing... unless Layton was talking about how he'd ambushed the sheriff to save her. "Did you see Sheriff Gillette at the Buckrail?"

"'Course I did. Had to put up the horses and park the rig, didn't I?"

"I don't know what he told you, but..."

"He told me all I needed to hear. The law is looking for this man."

Eric raised his hands to the level of his ears and stood straight. "Maybe I can—"

"You shut your mouth, boy."

Sarah gasped. For a moment, she thought Layton was going to pull the trigger. She held her breath.

"I ain't listening to anything you have to say, after what you did. You move again, and you won't be alive to say another word."

Sarah tried to angle her body between Layton and Eric. She had to convince her foreman to lower the rifle. She had to make him understand. "Eric only did what he did to save me."

Layton stared at her, brows arched. "Did

what he did? For you? I don't think you know what's gone down today, Sarah."

"The sheriff. He was asking me questions. He threatened me. He was going to hurt me, Layton. Eric stopped him."

He shook his head. "What I'm talking about don't have much to do with the sheriff. It's Randy, Sarah. He's dead."

Even though Sarah had spent the last hours dwelling on her brother's loss, hearing Layton say the words out loud jolted through her as if she was experiencing them for the first time. She swallowed and willed herself not to begin crying anew. "I know."

"There's more. More that you don't know."

Her head felt light, like it was spinning. She needed to ask, to find out what else had happened. But she couldn't manage to squeeze the words past her lips.

"It's him, Sarah." Layton tipped the brim of his Stetson at Eric. "He's the one who did it. He killed your brother in cold blood."

"No. No. Listen, Layton—"

"I'll listen. Long as you need me to. First I got to call the sheriff."

"No, please. Wait. Just for a second. You don't understand."

"I think I'm understanding everything just fine. He's wanted for murder. Your brother's murder. There's a statewide manhunt."

A manhunt. For a fugitive. Sarah felt dizzy. So much for convincing other law enforcement agencies to help. The sheriff had beaten them to it. But maybe she could convince Layton to at least give Eric a chance to get away while he could. "Please, Layton. For me."

Layton paused. His breath fogged the air before dissipating into the night.

"Talk to me. Inside. Alone." She glanced at Eric. She could tell by his wary expression, he was worried about letting her out of his sight. Despite herself, a warm flutter centered in her chest. She pulled in a sharp breath of cold night air. "It will just take a minute. Then you can do what you need to do."

Layton focused on Eric and frowned. "He's not going anywhere."

"He won't." She exchanged looks with Eric, willing him to see she was giving him a chance to flee.

Layton shook his head slowly. "I ain't taking the chance that he'll run off." He motioned for Eric to walk toward the trailer door with a wave of his rifle.

"What are you going to do?"

He eyed a lariat that was laying on the steps leading to the door, as if he'd dropped it when he'd seen them approaching his home. "I'm going to make sure he doesn't sneak away before our talk is over."

"This isn't necessary, Layton. I'm not going to run off and leave Sarah here."

She tried not to think about how he'd done exactly that just three months ago, but some bitter remnant inside her couldn't help taking note. It figured that when his leaving finally made sense, Eric resisted the urge. "Please, Layton. He won't leave."

Layton dropped his gaze to the ground. "Take off your boots. Socks, too."

Eric glanced at Sarah, then knelt and did as Layton ordered. He tucked the socks into his boots and stood barefoot on the rocky ground.

"Bring those along, will you, Sarah?" Layton asked, his stare not wavering from Eric. "I'll be keeping an eye on you, Lander. You wander out of the light here, and you're game during hunting season, as far as I'm concerned. Understand?"

"Understand." Eric met Sarah's eyes and he mouthed, *Be careful*.

Sarah focused on Layton. She'd known him

most of her life. Layton was like a second father to her. No, more than that. He was far more attentive and caring than her own father had ever been. Layton wouldn't hurt her. He wouldn't turn her over to the sheriff. He couldn't.

Unease fluttered over her skin like the cold wind. She followed him into the trailer, carrying Eric's hiking boots in her hand. Once the screen door slammed behind her, she set the boots on the floor and faced Layton.

The foreman closed the solid door and stepped to the living room window. Watching Eric outside, he lowered the rifle, pointing the barrel at the floor, and slipped his finger out of the trigger guard. "That man killed your brother, Sarah."

"That's what the sheriff told you?"

"Not just him. It's been all over the news. Like I said, there's a statewide manhunt. We have to call the sheriff. Report that he's here."

"Eric didn't kill Randy."

"I figured you'd say that."

"He didn't."

"Were you there?"

"No."

He let out a breath. "Then you don't really know what happened."

"Neither do you."

"The sheriff does. They have forensics people. They found his hunting rifle."

"Eric's?"

"That's what Sheriff Gillette said. They think it's the murder weapon, Sarah."

"No. It can't be. Or at least Eric wasn't the one who fired it."

"They found his truck at the ranch. Towed it away for testing. It had blood in it."

"His head was bleeding. Eric didn't kill Randy." Sarah had to find a way to make Layton listen. He didn't understand. How could he? He hadn't seen the sheriff's desperation when he didn't get the answers he expected. He didn't know what the man was willing to do to her. What he'd almost done. "It's the sheriff, Layton. Two of his deputies shot Randy. The sheriff himself threatened to hit me."

Layton focused his full attention on her. "He…what did he do?"

"He handcuffed me and asked me questions about Randy. Where he was going. What I knew." She held up her hands to show him the bruises on her wrists, starting to purple.

"And what did you tell him?"

"That I didn't know anything. I mean, I knew

he was climbing with Eric. That's all he told me. But Sheriff Gillette didn't believe me."

"Did he hurt you?"

"No. No. Eric got there first. But if he hadn't jumped Gillette, I don't know what would have happened."

Layton stared out the window. Although he focused on Eric, who was standing unmoving within the circle of light glowing from above the door, his thoughts seemed far away.

Maybe she was reaching him. "If Eric's rifle was used to shoot Randy, then someone else was firing it. One of the deputies."

Layton rubbed his chin between fingers and thumb. "You really believe him?"

"I do."

"You believed him last winter."

Sarah's cheeks heated. She'd thought she'd found something with Eric. Something that would grow. Something that would last. She had been wrong. Although she'd never told Layton exactly how she felt about Eric, it didn't surprise her that he knew. He had to have seen it, in her happiness when she and Eric were together and in her devastation after Eric had broken it off. "I know I was wrong then. But I'm not wrong now. Eric is not a murderer."

"If he's as innocent as you say, he should turn himself in."

She didn't want to argue with him. Not when she knew she couldn't win. Layton trusted the law. The system had delivered justice when his daughter was killed all those years ago. It was no surprise he wanted to trust it now. "That's up to Eric."

He shook his head. "Maybe so. But if you're with him, you're in danger. The sheriff will think you're part of Lander's plan. That you're working with him or something."

"I am working with him. I'm working to find the truth."

"I don't want you hurt, Sarah. You're my family…like my own daughter."

An ache hollowed out at the base of her throat. It was true. Since Layton had lost his daughter, he'd adopted Sarah in every way that mattered. He'd watched over her, cared for her, been there for her, while her parents were too wound up in their war with one another to give much thought to their children. Sometimes she couldn't help but feeling that Layton's attention had saved her from following Randy's self-destructive path. "I know. I feel the same way about you."

"Then do as I say. Let the sheriff take Lander. Let the law sort things out. You can stay here with me. I'll protect you."

That had always been the bottom line for Layton. Protecting her. But he hadn't seen the sheriff's face, his desperation, his refusal to let anything stand in his way. Layton was a good man, but he didn't have any special kind of pull in the county. As the owner of a decent-sized cattle operation, she had more political muscle than he did. If the sheriff continued to come after her, as he'd already started, a man like Layton couldn't stop him, no matter what the foreman wanted to believe.

And she didn't believe for one second that the law would sort anything out. The sheriff couldn't have Eric and her testifying in court. He would never let things go that far. "I can't do that, Layton. I can't sit by and let you turn Eric over to the sheriff."

The older man looked at her. His fence-straight frame seemed to droop in front of her eyes. "Don't throw your life away on someone like him."

"The sheriff is framing Eric, Layton. He might even have him killed. Just like he and his men killed Randy."

The foreman shook his head. "I know you loved your brother, but he chose the type of life he wanted. He hung out with a rough crowd. Scum. Keith and Glenn saw his truck down to the Full Throttle the very afternoon he got out of jail. You hang out with people like that, you become one of 'em, Sarah. Any one of those friends of Randy's might have killed him at any time."

She could feel the tears again, that pressure, that sting. He wasn't listening. "But Eric saw—"

"That's just it. Eric saw. You don't know what reasons he might have to lie. The sheriff and deputies shooting people down? That's pretty hard to believe."

"You didn't see the sheriff the way I did. He's convinced I know whatever it is Randy was looking for. He's not just going to let me walk away, even if I am not with Eric."

"Do you know what he's looking for?"

"No. And neither does Eric."

Layton looked down at the floor. He stroked the stock of his rifle with his thumb.

Did he believe her? She'd like to think so, but she couldn't tell. "We need to find out what's going on. We need to learn the truth."

"Seems like the truth is staring you in the face, but you don't want to see it."

She was sure it did seem that way to him. She shook her head.

"You stay with him and you're putting yourself in danger, Sarah."

"I might be in danger, but it's not coming from Eric."

"You're sure of that?"

"I'm sure."

Her stomach tightened, making her feel sick. She had to think of something to convince him. Her and the ranch were all Layton really cared about. Maybe that was the key. "I'll make you a deal."

He tilted his head and looked at her out of the corner of his eye.

"If you don't call the sheriff, if you forget Eric was here, I'll stay here with you."

"You're asking a lot, Sarah."

"Please, Layton. The sheriff is corrupt. I'm afraid if he catches Eric, he'll kill him."

He shook his head. "Sheriff Gillette believes in justice. He's a lawman to his bones."

Despite his obvious doubts, Layton would never believe the sheriff was a murderer. He had no reason to distrust the law and every reason to distrust Eric. She doubted anything she said could make him change his mind. But maybe she didn't have to. "All he needs is time to find out what's going on. Time to discover why Randy died. Listen to me. Please, Layton."

He stared over the top of her head and out the window. Finally he gave a hesitant nod. "I'll always listen to you. I just don't agree that letting a murderer go is a good idea."

"Whether he finds something at the place where Randy was headed or not, he'll turn himself in, just not to Sheriff Gillette."

Layton watched her under bushy brows. "And you can promise me that?"

"Yes." She wasn't sure how Eric would feel about her promise. But he'd have to understand she was struggling to do the best she could…and she had to pray it was the right thing.

Layton tilted his head to the side, a gesture that usually showed he was softening.

"So you won't call the sheriff?"

"I have to report Lander was here, Sarah. It's against the law to keep something like that to myself."

"But you'll wait a bit? Give him a chance to find out why Randy was killed?"

He let out a groan and shook his head. "God help me."

Sarah's whole body felt spongy with relief.

She'd hoped she could explain the situation to Layton, make him understand, but she'd had her doubts. And while she wouldn't be surprised if he called the sheriff first thing in the morning, at least Eric would have a head start.

Unfortunately that wasn't all he needed. "I hate to ask you for more, Layton, but…"

"What is it?"

"Can Eric borrow some supplies and equipment?"

A chuckle rumbled low in his chest. He shook his head, not in a way that indicated he was turning her down, but in an "I can't believe you'd ask" sort of way.

"You can tell the sheriff he stole it."

"What does he need?"

"Water, food, climbing gear."

"Fine."

"And the ATV?"

"That belongs to the ranch, and you know it. Where I'm sitting, he's going to have to ask *you* if he wants to borrow that."

"Thank you, Layton. Thank you so much." She reached up to him and he gathered her into a hug.

The warm scent of pipe smoke and fresh air made her throat clench. And for a moment she felt like she was a little girl once more, with

Layton always there to watch out for her. Always there to make things right.

Too bad this time the problem was far too big for him to make it go away.

ERIC SORTED THROUGH ROPES, harnesses and assortment of carabiners and other equipment Layton stored in the barn. Jamming the gear into a pack alongside protein bars, water and a small first-aid kit, he tried to push the myriad of what-ifs to the back of his mind. He'd cleaned the cut on his head, even if it did still throb like a son of a bitch. Now that he had transportation, food, water and most of the equipment he needed, he was in good shape to make the trek to Saddle Horn Ridge. That didn't mean he was eager to leave Sarah behind.

The ranch foreman had promised to keep their secret and keep Sarah safe, but Eric still felt uneasy about the whole thing. He never could read Layton. The foreman was good at keeping his feelings squirreled away, at least those other than contempt for Eric. But though Sarah trusted him, Eric didn't.

Sarah stuck her head into the tack room. Their clothes had been dried, and she was wearing an oversized coat provided by Layton.

Her black-and-white shadow padded into the barn and laid down at her feet. "The ATV is gassed up and ready."

So this was goodbye. He felt a little shaky in the pit of his stomach. "You're sure Layton isn't phoning the sheriff as we speak, so he can head me off at the ridge?"

"He promised."

"And you believe him."

"He's never let me down before."

"Good to know."

"Eric?"

A little jolt shimmered up his spine at her tone. "What is it?"

"I…" She pressed her lips together as if trying to keep words from slipping past. She raised her hand to touch him, then let it fall to her side. "Good luck is all."

He reached out a hand and skimmed it down her arm. What he wouldn't give to be able to pull her into his arms right now. Take her in a kiss. Show her all the things he couldn't let himself feel, couldn't let himself want. He blew out a breath and pushed his clamoring feelings down. "Thanks."

The tack room door flew open. Layton pushed inside. His gray hair was tousled, as if he'd been running agitated hands through it. His eyes gaped wide with alarm. "You got to get out of here. Now."

Sarah stared at him, blood draining from her face and forcing her lips taut. "The sheriff?"

"He's on his way."

Eric finished shoving the equipment into the pack and yanked the zipper home. "How did he know we're here?"

"A neighbor? A hunch? I don't know. But he just called me. Started asking questions." Layton motioned for them to move, scooping the air with his hands.

A neighbor? Layton didn't have any neighbors, not for miles. Of course it probably didn't take a big guess for the sheriff to figure Sarah would go to the closest place she could for help. Layton's. Not that the reason mattered. The only thing important now was getting the hell out of here. He was grateful Layton tipped him off. "What did you tell him?"

"That I didn't know what he was talking about, but I don't think he believed me. And Sarah?"

She looked up at the older man.

"What you said before about the sheriff? It's true. He isn't just after Lander. He wants you, too. You'll have to go with Lander after all."

Sarah nodded, that determined set returning to her jaw.

Eric stifled a protest. As much as leaving Sarah bothered him, having her go with him to the ridge was not what he would choose. "It's too risky."

Layton gave him a sideways glance. "Believe me, it's not my choice. I don't want her near you."

Sarah nailed him with a determined glare. "The sheriff's on his way. I'm going."

Eric hesitated, then forced a nod. He couldn't very well leave her here. Not with the sheriff bearing down on her. No matter what happened, he had to make sure she was safe.

Shoving extra climbing equipment into the backpack, he glanced down at Radar. The dog had been lying flat out on his side a moment ago, but now he crouched, staring at Sarah as if waiting for a command so he could fly into action and fix everything the humans were upset about.

Eric didn't want to say anything. Sarah had lost so much in the past hours. Randy. Her belief in the law. Every shred of security she'd known. He knew that to her, giving up Radar would feel like the ultimate blow. But there was nothing he could do. "What about your dog?"

Sarah sucked in a breath. She ran her fingers over the black-and-white head.

Layton rested a comforting hand on her shoulder. "Can't take a dog on an ATV."

She nodded and swiped at her cheeks with the back of one hand. It didn't work. Tears wound down her cheeks, reflecting the barn light in mirrored rivulets. "Will you take him?"

"You know I will."

She parted her lips to speak, then covered them with a hand as if holding back a sob.

Layton rubbed a hand over her shoulder. "I'll stall the sheriff as long as I can."

"Thank you, Layton." Sarah reached up and hugged him.

When she released him, he shooed them out the door. "Hurry."

Layton grabbed the backpack and helped Sarah slip it on her shoulders while Eric climbed on the all-terrain vehicle. He started it up, the engine buzzing loudly in the night. Sarah climbed on behind.

The foreman raised a hand in a wave as they sped away, his eyes glistening in the yard light.

Chapter Six

Each jolt of the ATV over rock and sage shuddered up Eric's spine and throbbed through his head, as if the very landscape was beating on him. The engine roared loud in the quiet night. At least it had stopped raining. With any luck, the snow wouldn't be too deep, at least not at lower elevations like Saddle Horn Ridge. But although the calendar said early June, spring had yet to arrive in many parts of the mountains.

He focused on the wrap of Sarah's arms around his waist, the warmth of her thighs pressing to the back of his. Even though the rain was long since over, the night air was downright cold as it rushed past. He could feel her shiver as she pressed against him. At least she now had a coat, thanks to Layton.

Obviously the foreman shared Eric's need to protect her. The urge never made sense. She was the strongest woman he'd ever known. She took care of others, animal and human alike. She never seemed to need anyone.

Of course, the jumble of feelings that overwhelmed him whenever he was around Sarah never made a lot of sense. In the rest of his life, he was controlled, logical. But as soon as he saw the way she tilted her chin, heard her voice or touched her skin, he lost all reason. All he could think of was her.

He had to keep his mind clear if he wanted to get out of this mess.

They reached the mountains just as the first evidence of dawn started glowing from the east. As the light grew, driving became easier. The ATV could carry them farther up the mountain than his truck had allowed, cutting hours off the trip he and Randy had taken on foot. Good thing. After a night of no sleep and a lifetime's worth of trauma, the only thing keeping either of them going was adrenaline. And who knew how long that could last?

The ATV bucked at every bump. The pitch grew steeper. Eric settled into a switchback trail nearby guest ranches used to take tourists through the area on horseback. They wove back and forth up the side of the slope, until the pitch grew too steep and the trail circled back. Stopping the ATV behind a jut of rock, Eric switched off the engine. "We're going to have to go the rest of the way on foot."

Sarah nodded and released his waist. She swung a leg over the seat and dismounted.

Cool air fanned over his back where her warmth had been. For a moment, he wanted nothing more than to have her back on the seat behind him, arms circling his waist.

Stupid.

He climbed off the ATV. His hands still vibrated from the feel of the handlebars. His ears buzzed with silence, now that the roar of the engine was gone. He focused on Sarah. Her skin was the color of aspen bark. Dark circles cupped under chocolate eyes that glistened with fatigue. She was far more exhausted than he'd even guessed. "Take a few minutes and sit down."

"I'm fine." She raised her chin in that way he'd once thought was sexy.

Now it struck him as nothing but stubborn. "You look like you're about to keel over."

She nodded her head toward the east. The glow of sunlight pinked the horizon. "The sun is going to be up any second. We don't have time to sit down."

She was right. As much as she needed to rest, they couldn't afford the delay. It had taken them a good long time to make it to the base of Saddle Horn Ridge. Pickups traveling paved roads would make it here a lot faster, although they'd have to cover more miles and couldn't drive as far up the mountainside. Unfortunately that small time advantage would be eaten up by the detour Eric planned to take. They needed every second they could get. "We'll keep going then. But I'll carry the pack."

She shrugged the backpack off her shoulders and handed it to him.

The pack was heavy in his hand, weighed down with harnesses and ropes, water and food. He slung it onto his back. "Let's go."

He stepped off the switchback trail and started picking his way over sage and around rock. Most of mountain climbing was a matter of walking uphill. It didn't involve ropes or vertical rock faces. It was about hiking, pure and simple. But that didn't mean it was the same thing as following a trail. Eric scanned the terrain ahead, aware of every rock and crevasse and ripple of the wind. Off-trail hiking was about being present, being aware. Of the surroundings, of animals, of the weather, of the capabilities of one's own body. It was about being awake in the present and being able to guess the future. And guiding meant he was responsible for Sarah as well.

The sun warmed their backs as it rose in the sky, beating down strong, even though the mountains still boasted a good amount of snow along their peaks. They worked their way through vegetation raging from the ever-present sage to tall stands of lodgepole pine and subalpine fir. The roar of a waterfall hung in the thinning air, though the creek itself was over a mile away.

Finally Saddle Horn Ridge loomed above them, stretching between two peaks. The ridge wasn't a common tourist destination, but the few guides working the area knew it was there. Most of the area itself was flat and sheltered from sometimes brutal mountain winds, an ideal spot for camping. On one side, a rock formation rose. A shifted slab of rock capped the top of the formation, giving it the appearance of the horn on a western saddle.

On one end of the long ridge, a vertical rock face rose nearly to the ridge itself. Made of hard, volcanic rock, like the rest of the Absaroka Range, this was one of the best and least known climbing areas north of the Tetons.

It was also the cliff he and Randy had been scaling when the deputies had opened fire.

Eric turned away from the stretch of rock and started through a long stand of lodgepole pine.

"Where are you going?"

"We'll circle to the other end of the ridge. Most of the terrain is hikable on that side."

"Won't that take a lot longer?" She tilted her face to the east, no doubt checking the position of the sun.

"A little. But it's easier. Multipitch climbs can be slow, tough going."

"You don't think I can do it."

Under normal circumstances, he might let her. She was pretty advanced. If she was in practice, she could probably handle it. They'd done some climbing together last September before the snow hit. Before he realized how important to him she was becoming. But circumstances were different now. "It's not a simple climb. We've both been through a lot in the past few hours."

"I told you, I'm fine. I can make it."

He hadn't believed her then, and he didn't believe her now. But her obvious fatigue wasn't the only reason he wanted to avoid this stretch. Just the sight of that rock face made a shudder travel through him and his head ache to high heaven. "We'll go through the pass and up the other side. It won't take much longer."

"But it will take longer. Do you really think we can afford that extra time?"

He didn't know. He was surprised they hadn't heard vehicles yet. Or helicopters. But to lead Sarah up that face? "We'll move fast. A climb like that is too dangerous."

"And letting the sheriff catch up to us isn't?"

"I'm not going to let you get caught on that face…."

She narrowed her eyes.

He pulled in a breath and gritted his teeth. He'd said too much. Way more than he should have. "Let's move. Now."

"This is the spot, isn't it?" She turned away from him and peered up at the rock face.

He started walking, heading for the pass.

"It's the spot where Randy…"

He slowed his steps. The pain in her words hollowed out a pit below his rib cage. He turned to face her and reached out a hand. "Come on. We'll follow the pass. It will be better."

"Where? Where did it happen?"

"Sarah, come on."

"Tell me. Please."

With that last whispered word, he felt the walls inside him crumble. A torrent of pain and regret filled his throat.

PRESSURE BUILT AROUND the edges of Sarah's eyes and stung through her sinuses. "Please, Eric. I have to know." She'd never understood the need of survivors to mark the spot where a loved one died. Every time she passed a cross on the side of the highway or flowers woven into a chain-link fence, she'd felt uneasy, as if she was witnessing a very personal pain, something that should be shielded from the public.

She understood now.

She needed to know exactly where Randy had taken his last breath. She needed to mark the spot, if only in her mind, in order to make any of it feel real.

He watched her for what had to be a full minute. "About three quarters of the way up. See the shelf of rock?"

She followed the direction of his pointing finger. "Near the top of those trees?"

"Yes."

She saw it. What looked like a smear of something brown on the stone. A trick of the noon sun...or her brother's blood? She couldn't tell.

Shivers fanned out over her skin. Her chest heaved in a barely controlled sob. She half expected him to still be there. Hanging in his climbing harness. Or lying in the short slope of scree at the bottom of the rock face. But she knew he wouldn't be. He would be at the morgue, his body dissected, his wounds used as evidence to frame Eric for his murder. "Was he in pain?"

"No…no." His voice hitched.

She could tell by his hesitation that wasn't entirely true.

She closed her eyes, trying to block the tears. Randy was gone. Murdered on this spot. And now nothing was left but to find out why. And make sure the same fate didn't fall on Eric or her…or their unborn child.

Nausea swirled in the pit of her stomach. She hadn't suffered morning sickness for a couple of weeks now, but it seemed a touch had caught up to her in the stress of the past hours. Maybe it had nothing to do with the baby. Maybe it was seeing the spot where Randy died. Or leaving Radar behind with Layton. Or maybe the confusion of all that had happened.

"Sarah. Is there something…"

She took a deep breath and braced herself before turning back to Eric.

His eyes focused on her belly.

She hadn't realized she was shielding her middle with her forearm. But she could tell by the expression on his face he had. And along with probably the dozen other signals she'd subconsciously given, he had a guess as to what the protective gesture meant.

Her throat went dry. "I was going to tell you."

"You're pregnant." He brought his eyes up to her face. For a long time, he just watched her. Struggling to make sense of her words, searching for words of his own, she didn't know. But just as she was about to break the silence, he nodded. "It's mine."

His voice sounded dead, void of emotion, and somehow that bothered her more than the anger and betrayal she'd imagined he'd feel in all the times she'd played this scenario out in her imagination. "Yes. The baby is yours."

"How far along?"

"Four months. I found out shortly after we... after you..."

"Left."

"Yes."

"Why didn't you tell me then? Call me?"

"I was going to. Really I was...but..."

"But what?"

She'd made excuses to herself for months. She didn't want to try to make them now. Not when she knew the reason she hadn't told him. "I was afraid."

"Of what? You had to know I'd marry you."

She flinched and took a step backward. Of course, she knew. It was the right thing to do. And Eric would never walk away from doing the right thing.

And that was exactly what she feared most.

SARAH STARED AT ERIC as if he'd just said exactly the wrong thing. Slowly, she shook her head. "You don't want to get married."

Eric couldn't disagree. "It wasn't in my plans. But some things are more important than plans." He closed his eyes. Dizziness swept over him in a sudden, stomach-wrenching bout of vertigo. He pulled in a breath and beat back the sensation. He wasn't a man who ran out on his responsibilities. Ever. If he wasn't sure he could come through, he didn't take it on in the first place. He approached things in a controlled way, a logical way. Reason instead of emotion. He just had to get used to the idea and the weak, shaky feeling in the pit of his stomach would go away.

Wouldn't it?

"I'm not going to marry you, Eric."

He opened his eyes and stared at Sarah. He couldn't have heard her right. "What?"

"I don't want to marry you."

He shook his head. "But you're pregnant."

"And people have babies without getting married all the time. Really, it's fine."

How could she say that? "No. It's not fine. I'm tired of you saying everything is fine." If there was anything he knew about any of what he'd had sprung on him the past two days, it was that absolutely nothing was fine.

"A couple of months ago, you told me you didn't even want to date anymore. Now you have a pressing desire to marry me?"

"Things have changed."

"Nothing's changed."

"How do you figure that?"

"You just think marrying me is something you have to do. Your duty or whatever. Well, I'm telling you it isn't."

His duty. That was how he felt, she was right. But that didn't mean she could absolve him of it. "I *want* to do it."

She tilted her chin down and looked up at him. "Well, I don't."

He looked away. He couldn't blame her. He

knew when he'd broken things off she'd assumed he didn't care about her. And for the ease of the breakup, he'd let her believe that. He'd told himself the truth was far too complicated. Compared to the mess they were in now, it was amazingly simple. Not that it mattered. Not anymore. "So where does that leave us?"

"Same place as before. We find whatever it is that's up on that ridge and we use it to try to get our lives back."

Their lives. He knew she meant their separate lives. But to him, that was no longer an option.

"They're here."

He followed her gaze to where the white dot of an SUV bounced over rutted gravel road, slowly making its way to the head of the switchback trail.

SARAH KNEW ERIC DIDN'T want to get married. Hell, he probably knew it, too. But that split second when she told him she wouldn't consider wedlock, the look of rejection on his face felt good.

She wasn't sure if that officially made her a horrible person, but…whatever.

She shook her head and found her next foothold. As satisfying as revenge felt, her reason for turning him down went a lot deeper. As much as she wanted to go back to the way things were before Eric left, before Randy died, before her life totally fell apart, when he'd asked her to marry him, the feeling that he was merely doing his duty hit her like a kick to the gut. No, more like a void. An emptiness that could never be filled. There was no use pretending things might have worked out between them if she'd played things differently, said different words, batted her eyes just so. There was no more pretending at all.

The bottom line was that Eric didn't love her. If he had, he never would have walked away. And she wasn't going to marry someone without love.

Period.

Now all that was left was the task ahead. Finding whatever had gotten Randy killed and using it to clear their names.

She shoved all other thoughts from her mind and concentrated on fitting her fingers into a jam-crack in the short rock face at the top of the ridge that Eric hadn't been able to avoid letting her climb.

Last summer, Eric had said she was a natural climber. She was patient, and she relied on her legs to make the climb, using her hands only for balance. That might have been the case back then. Today she felt clumsy and hurried and her arms ached with exertion. And every time her tummy rubbed against the rock, all she could think of was the danger to her baby if she fell.

Concentrate.

She placed her boot on a block. Keeping her heels low, she took weight onto the foot and pushed herself up. Eric took up the slack in the belaying rope. She pulled herself to the top of the ridge and shifted her weight to her elbows.

"You got it." Eric's voice sounded in her ears, right above her head. "Now just bring your foot up, and you're home free."

Home free. She knew it was merely a saying, but she couldn't help the hitch in her stomach all the same. She might be home free as far as this climb went. But the situation they were in stretched in front of them like the most rugged of mountain ranges. And even if they could get through all the obstacles before them, she might never be home free again.

She raised her foot to the ledge and thrust her body up onto the top of the ridge. For a second, she just lay there, her muscles quivering under her skin. Then she pulled herself into a sitting position.

Saddle Horn Ridge.

All around her mountains rose above them, jutting their snow-topped peaks into the sky. Rock and stretches of lodgepole pine seemed to go on forever. "Beautiful."

"It is." Eric quickly looked away from her and out at the gully cutting below the other side of the ridge.

She watched him for a second, like he'd been watching her. Now that he knew about the baby, now that they'd gotten the marriage discussion out of the way, they seemed as awkward as strangers. "Do you see anyone?"

A light swirl of wind blew past her ears and swept away his answer, but she could read from his body language that he hadn't. She scanned the area with her own eyes. No sign of human life other than them. But then, Eric had led them on such a winding path up to the ridge, she was no longer sure in which direction to look.

She scooped in a long breath. "Now what?"

"Now we look around."

He moved to the far edge of the ridge, where the rock rose in a column and formed a shape some explorer must have thought looked like a saddle horn. He peered down, not moving except for the light breeze rifling his hair.

She thrust herself up from her resting place. "If the sheriff was worried about Randy finding money or drugs, why didn't he just come up here and take it himself?"

"Maybe he tried."

Something in the tone of his voice stopped Sarah as effectively as if he'd grabbed her. Pulse thumping, she willed her wobbly legs to carry her along the rocky ridge toward the base of the saddle horn.

The area was wider than it seemed, flat, but on all sides the plunge was straight down. And even though she logically knew she was in no danger, she couldn't shake the feeling that the wind could push her off her perch at any moment and toss her to the rock below, even though there was surprisingly little wind. "What is it?"

"Not what we thought." He pointed to a fissure in the rock.

Deep in the shadows, she could see light tan against dark. Something with a trunk, with arms... "A person?"

"A body. And judging from the shape he's in, he might have been stuck in that crevasse a good long while."

Chapter Seven

"Randy was looking for a dead body?"

Eric felt as shaken by the discovery as Sarah sounded. "He was looking for something valuable enough to pay off his debt."

"So what makes this guy valuable?"

Shielding his eyes from the sun, he tried to get a better look. What he wouldn't give for a pair of binoculars. "Maybe there's something valuable on the body."

"Like money or drugs. But what would he be doing with money or drugs out here? And how did he die? Fall?"

"Good questions." And ones he couldn't answer. "I'm going to rappel down. Take a look."

Sarah inched closer to the edge and craned her neck. Swaying a little, she clamped her hand to her stomach.

"Are you okay?"

"Just a little dizzy."

"Heights do that to some people."

"I climbed up all right."

"Not the same as rappelling down."

"I guess not." She took a deep breath, as if she could push the vertigo down with will-power alone.

"You don't have to do it. I'll go alone. You stay up here and watch for the sheriff's men."

She nodded, as if eager to jump at the chance to sit this one out.

She had to be tired. Even though she was in great shape, and they'd avoided the worst of the climbs, scaling rock worked different muscles than ranch work. Add that to a sleepless night and extreme stress and anyone would be dragging. He couldn't even begin to imagine adding the strain of being pregnant.

Pregnant. He still couldn't wrap his mind around the fact that he and Sarah were going to have a baby. He felt excited about the idea on some level, but jangled and confused at the same time. And not just about the baby. Seeing Sarah again, being near her, made him feel like a broken compass with no sense of north.

He needed distance. A chance to think things

over logically, approach the whole thing with a clear mind.

But in order to get control of that situation, he needed to get out of this one first.

Using a tape sling, he set up an anchor around a solid rock formation. He ran a coil of rope through a carabiner, forming a pulley. After formulating a plan and giving Sarah a quick lesson in threading the rope through a descender, he started down the side of the cliff. It took mere seconds to rappel down the thirty-foot drop. As soon as his feet hit the narrow shelf of rock on the edge of the crevasse, a thick sweet smell touched his senses.

Apparently the body hadn't been here as long as he'd thought. He crouched down to take a look at the dead man.

From the top of the ridge, all he'd seen was the clothing. A shearling coat sun-bleached and ratty from the elements. A pair of Wranglers. Cowboy boots. And at first that was all he could see. Wedged about four feet down into the crevasse, the body was angled head down. Eric focused on the boots. Great for riding, but not something a hiker or climber would wear—he thought of Sarah's footwear—not by choice, anyway. But the popularity of Wrangler jeans and shearling coats in this part of the country meant the rest told him little about who this man was and how he had ended up here.

Or what of value he might have.

He bridged the narrow crack, one foot on either side, and settled in as low as he could get. Reaching down, he patted the coat pockets. Empty. He grasped the bottom hem and yanked it up, exposing a stained shirt. There was little left of the guy except clothing and bones, but a strong wave of odor still wafted up at him and tainted the air around him. His stomach bucked for a moment, then calmed. He breathed through his mouth and prodded further. All the man's pockets were empty. Not even a wallet.

A leather belt loosely circled the man's waist. Judging from the circumference, it had likely propped up a good-sized belly, back when their mystery man was alive. An ornate belt buckle fastened the ends of the tooled leather.

Eric grabbed a small flashlight from his pack and focused its beam on the buckle. Exposure to the elements had tarnished the silver to a dull gray, but Eric could still make out the inscription among the curlycues surrounding a man on a bucking horse—*Cody Nite Rodeo Bareback Champion, 1978.*

He skimmed the beam up the torso. What he'd thought was the man's head when looking down from the ridge above was really his shoulder. The crevasse cut deep into rock, narrowing on its way down to blackness. One arm reached down, but he could see nothing below, no bag or pack or anything that could be considered valuable. Below the shoulder, the skull wedged between rock, only a small tuft of gray hair clung to shriveled skin and bone.

Eric ran the questions the sheriff had asked Sarah through his mind. Even if Gillette knew the area to look, he would have only been able to see the body from directly above the crevasse. And even if he'd known exactly where it was, it would have been difficult to move a body wedged deep like this.

"Who in the hell are you, Mr. Rodeo Champion? And why are you so valuable?"

Of course, dental records or DNA could tell them who he was. Not that he nor Sarah could waltz into the Wyoming crime lab with a sample. Even a private lab would ask too many questions, provided they asked questions at all and didn't merely call the police.

And in light of what Layton had told them,

they couldn't rely on police to do anything but arrest them and ship them back to Sheriff Gillette.

He moved the light beam over the skull, stopping on a spot at the back of the head.

Wait.

Throat dry, Eric adjusted his position and leaned as far into the crevasse as he dared. He scanned the skull again, raking the beam slowly over hair and bone. There it was. A hole marked the cranium like a perfect dark circle, just an inch or so behind the ear.

He pulled in a breath of foul air. There wasn't any treasure at all at the end of this treasure hunt. The deputies hadn't been hiding a stash of money or drugs. They'd been trying to cover up a murder.

The rope around Eric's waist jolted.

Sarah's signal. He looked up. The men must be getting close. Too close. He needed to get back up to the top of that ridge and he needed to do it now. He reached for the rodeo belt buckle, unhooked it and gave it a hard pull. The leather started slipping through the denim loops, then caught. He tugged harder.

No good. It held fast.

Twisting the buckle upside down, he fumbled for the snaps holding leather to silver. He popped one snap, then the other. Slipping buckle free of belt and body, he stuffed it into his pack.

The rope tugged again, more frantic. He needed to hurry. The thought of Sarah up on the ridge alone, frightened, facing down men with guns… He spun around. His foot skidded beneath him. He struggled for balance, grasped at rock for a hold. No good.

He plunged into the crevasse up to his waist. Damn.

The body's skull pressed against his thigh. The scent of decay coated the back of his throat. A wave of revulsion shuddered through him before he could take control.

Calm. Logical. Pull yourself out and get the hell up to that ridge.

He placed his palms on the edge of the crevasse. His forearms were already over the ledge, in a position where he could push himself over the rock instead of pull. He'd mantled more times than he could remember. Performing the move next to a dead body didn't change anything.

He pushed down with his hands and slung his left foot up onto the narrow ledge. Scooping in a breath through his mouth, he pushed upward.

His right foot didn't budge.

He tried again, giving it every ounce of strength he could muster. No good. His foot wouldn't move. A cold sweat blanketed him, thick as the odor of decay.

He was as stuck in the crevasse as the dead man.

SARAH TUGGED ON THE ROPE for a third time. What was taking Eric so long? The men had crested the point and had now disappeared behind a stand of lodgepole pine. She wasn't sure how long it would take for him to make the climb back up to the ridge and then for them to make their escape, but time seemed to be tightening at an alarming rate.

"Sarah."

She leaned over the edge.

Eric seemed to be standing in the crevasse next to the body. He hadn't moved, even though she'd warned him three times.

The beat of her pulse drowned out the whistle of wind in the rocks above.

Eric scooped the air with one arm.

At first she didn't understand what he was trying to tell her. The second time he made the gesture, his meaning dawned.

He was telling her she'd have to come down

to him. He was asking her to rappel down the sheer drop of rock.

A tremor seized low in her stomach. She looked back in the direction of the men. Eric must have figured out that he didn't have time to make the climb and then make their escape. Something had delayed him. Something was wrong.

She pulled in a breath of too thin air. She'd rappelled down a rock face before. She was the same person. She could do it again. But somehow every risk seemed to be bigger now, every possible danger more dire.

She glanced back at the path one more time. She couldn't see the men. Not yet. But they were coming. And they would be armed. If she wanted to think about danger, that was the direction from which it would come.

She grasped the rope Eric had used. Still threaded through the pulley he'd set up, the rope was now loose on Eric's end. He'd detached it from his harness, freed it for her. Hands shaking, she threaded it through the big circle of the descender. She looped it around the small end and clipped the device to her harness the way Eric had shown her.

So far, so good.

After checking the ropes, she stepped to the

edge. Eric's instructions rang in her ears. She had to trust her equipment, take her time. Breathe.

She leaned back and dug her heels into the rock. Her front hand shook, fingers aching. She forced her grip to loosen. Her right hand, resting along her thigh, was controlling the rope. She had to remember that. If she moved it to the side, the rope would slide through the descender. If she held it behind her back, the rope would stop.

She inched down the cliff, forcing herself to keep her eyes down, on the rock under her feet and the cliff below, and not on the ridge above. She leaned back, but not too far. She had to hurry, but not too much. Finally she could see the rock flatten into a narrow ledge.

"You got it," Eric's voice sounded from behind her.

One of the most welcome sounds she'd ever heard. She let the rope slide through her hands. Her feet rested on horizontal rock.

His hands steadied her hips. "Don't step back. Stay right where you are."

For a moment, she was content not to move. She just stood there, soaking in the solid feel of his touch. The smell of decay and tension and relief made her stomach swirl. She looked up at the cliff she'd just descended, half expecting to see men peering down at them, gun barrels leveled at their heads, although she knew they weren't that close. "They're on their way. I spotted them on the point, just where you said to look."

"We have a problem."

She turned around on the narrow ledge. He was standing waist-deep in a crevasse, just as it had seemed from above. And beside him, the body they'd spotted from above wedged a few feet deeper. She suppressed a shudder.

"My boot is jammed."

She looked down, following his leg to where it was swallowed by shadow cast by the narrowing slash in the rock. "Can you get it off?"

"I can't bend down to get it unlaced. The crevasse is too tight. I need your help." He pulled a knife from his belt and handed it to her. Blade tucked neatly into handle, the knife still looked brutal, the blade big enough to hack down a small tree. The olive drab handle looked military-serious. "The laces. Can you reach them? Cut them with this?"

"Not unless I stand on my head."

"Okay, then."

She eyed the crevasse, the body lodged beside Eric. The thought of diving headfirst into that confining space made sweat bloom damp on her skin. "I wasn't serious."

"I was. I'm not going to get out of here any other way."

She wiped her palms on her jeans and took the knife. "I hope I don't get sick."

His eyebrows turned down.

"Don't worry about it. I can do it. Just wanted to warn you."

"You sure?"

"Believe me, I'm used to it. I'm sure it will bother you more than it bothers me." She turned to face him on the ledge. He was so close to her. "As long as you can pull me back up."

He nodded, but he didn't have to. She knew he could. Eric was one of the strongest men she'd ever known. Rock climbing honed some brutal muscle tissue.

"You might want to breathe through your mouth."

Sarah tried not to look at the body. She scooped in a deep breath through tight lips. Leaning forward, she lowered her head in an awkward half headstand, half squat.

Eric's hands closed around her waist and he lifted her into the air. She stretched her arms out in front of her, the knife clutched in one fist.

He lowered her into the crevasse, her body sliding down his. Darkness closed around her. The odor of decay wrapped around her like a wet fog. She kept her eyes on Eric's boot, trying not to think too much about the skull just inches away.

The opening narrowed. Her face grew hot, blood rushing to her head. The weight of her stomach pressed into her throat. The urge to break out of here, scramble for light, for air, clawed inside her.

She had to hurry.

Locating a lace with one hand, she slipped the blade under and drew it upward. She jiggled the knife until the lace gave. She cut another, then clawed the rest loose with her fingers and pulled at the boot's tongue. She folded the knife and tapped Eric's leg.

He started to lift her upward. She hadn't yet emerged from the crevasse when she heard the first crack of gunfire reverberate off stone.

Chapter Eight

Nothing could get adrenaline pumping like a bullet screaming past a person's head.

Eric's arms shook as he lifted Sarah out of the crevasse. She wasn't that heavy. Not heavy at all, really. But slam after slam of adrenaline over the past hours was taking its toll.

His heart hammered against his ribs. This couldn't be happening again. Images flashed through his mind. The sick jolt of Randy's body. The animal look in his eyes. They way he slumped off the ridge and hung limp in his harness.

Think. He had to get Sarah out of here. He'd failed Randy. He wouldn't fail her.

Sarah and his child.

Setting her on the edge, he yanked his foot free from the boot and hefted himself up beside her.

Crack. A plume of dust exploded from rock.

A choked sound came from Sarah's throat.

Grabbing her hand, he flattened himself against the base of the cliff. She did the same. At this angle, even a few feet made a difference. Rock and the occasional straggly sage obscured them from above. It would be tough for the men on the ridge to pull off an accurate shot at this angle. Until they decided to rappel down the rock face as he and Sarah had. Or circle around the gentler slope to the other side of the ridge.

Or split up and try both.

Eric swallowed into a dust-dry throat. That's what he would do, if he were the hunter instead of the prey. It was the logical move. Come at them from both sides. Get into position before making his presence known.

Sarah pulled his hand, leading him back around the ridge the way they'd come. "Hurry. If they're up there, maybe we can reach the ATV before—"

"They'll be coming from both directions. We'll run right into them."

She stared at him a moment, processing his words or deciding whether or not to trust him, he wasn't sure. "So where do we go?" She searched his eyes, waiting for his answer.

Eric scanned the mountains that rose all

around them. To someone who hadn't spent the hours in these mountains that he had, the formations of rock, slopes of pine and peaks dusted with snow looked interchangeable. All beautiful, but one much like the other. For him, each mountain's shape and features felt as distinctive as human faces. And these particular faces were all well loved.

"That way." He pointed to the other side of the crevasse. The slope stretched bare and open for fifty yards then plunged into a stand of lodgepole pine.

But first, he needed to make things a little tougher for their pursuers and easier for themselves.

He grabbed the rope and gave it a good pull. It slid through the carabiner above and pooled at the base of the cliff. He coiled it as quickly as his hands would move. Taking the rope was time-consuming, he knew. But with the route he was planning to take, two ropes would be important. Hell, they'd be the difference between one of them making it or both.

Slipping the coil over his shoulder, he grabbed Sarah's hand once more. He nodded to the open landscape in front of them and the stand of lodgepole pine beyond. "We'll need to cross this stretch quickly. Once we get into cover, we'll be in good shape. But until then… we need to move fast. Keep down and stay with me. You think you're up to it?"

Holding her hand to her belly, she set her jaw and nodded. "Just tell me what to do." Her voice trembled, but there was a determination underneath it, a confidence in him he thought he'd never hear from her again. And despite the fact that he had little idea how he was going to get them out of this mess, her confidence that he'd find a way made him want to believe it, too. "On three, run."

"ONE."

Sarah gripped Eric's hand for all she was worth. She couldn't let herself think about what they were about to do. She just had to feel, trust.

"TWO."

She mimicked Eric's posture, knees bent, muscles coiled like springs. Time stretched forever, slow and painful. Finally he opened his lips a third time.

"Three."

They sprang over the crevasse and into the open, racing for the stand of pine. Her boots skidded on rock and tripped over prickly pear, but she kept her legs under her, kept them moving, kept hold of Eric's hand.

A crack echoed off stone. Another.

They plunged into the forest's edge. From the ridge the trees had appeared closer together. Dense. Now she could see how sparse the forest really was. Some pines ravaged by past fires were bare as matchsticks thrust into the sky. Others had needles, but were too young to provide cover.

They kept moving. Sarah's breath panted raw in her throat. She tried to make herself breathe deeply, sucking in all the oxygen she could with each breath, but still her lungs craved more.

Eric picked and dodged around rocks and through brush. Finally the forest grew darker, the understory more sparse until only a bed of dead needles cushioned the rocky soil beneath their feet.

Instead of stopping, Eric ran on. No longer a mad dash, but a steady jog. Sarah gamely kept up. The gunshots coming from the top of the ridge echoed in her ears. They were too close. Too real. Those moments before Eric had led her to shelter had scared her as she'd never been scared before, and every cell in her body seemed to still be shaking from it.

Her breathing settled into a steady rhythm. In

and out. In and out. Blood hummed through her arms and legs. Hair stuck to her face and neck, sweat slicking her skin.

They ran on, through forest then open space. They hiked over ridges and rappeled down steep slopes. By the time Sarah made it down the cliff near the waterfall, she was starting to feel like a pro. Either that or she was just so exhausted she was becoming delusional.

Her side stung with each breath as if a knife had been jabbed between her ribs. She swallowed into a dust-dry throat. "I have to stop. Just for a second."

Eric paused as if listening for the sound of pursuit. Finally he nodded and led her to the side of the stream. He handed her one of the water bottles Layton had provided and slugged back the other himself. Once they were empty, he refilled them from the stream, slipped them back into the pack and propped a hip on the slope of a felled log.

Even though the sharp pain in her lungs had lessened, Sarah's whole body still ached, and she knew if she sat for long each of those overtaxed muscles would stiffen, making things worse.

But a few minutes would be nice.

The sound of water washing over stone lulled

her like the mellow tones of New Age music. She breathed in the fresh tang of pine and plopped her elbows on her knees. "Did you find anything? You know, on the body?" They had been in such a hurry to escape the gunfire, she hadn't had a chance to ask until now.

"You mean like something on him that would carry stolen money or drugs? No."

She leaned forehead to hands. She'd hung everything on the hope they'd find something on the ridge. Something to explain why Randy was killed. Something to help them get out of this mess. "Then the hike up to Saddle Horn Ridge…it was all for nothing?"

"I wouldn't say that."

"We almost got killed, and we know nothing more now than we did before we climbed to the ridge."

He scanned the rough landscape around them, always on guard. "We know several things."

"Like what?" At the moment, she couldn't think of one.

"We know there's a body."

Yes, they knew that, all right. The rotting flesh, the sickening smell…she suppressed a shiver. "So? If he didn't have anything Randy could have thought was valuable enough to pay back his debt, we have no proof he's part of this at all. He might just be a hiker who fell."

"He was no hiker."

"How do you know?"

"First, he was wearing the wrong boots." He glanced down at the cowboy boots on her feet. "You know from experience that wouldn't be the first choice for a hike."

She couldn't disagree. She studied the confident line of his mouth. "I get the feeling there's more?"

"He was murdered."

The word sent a jolt of energy through her she didn't know she still possessed. "How do you know?"

"There was a bullet hole in the back of his skull. And…" He hefted the backpack up on the log beside him, unzipped it and pulled something out. He handed her a silver belt buckle.

"This is from the body?" She held it by the edges, balancing it between two fingers, not sure she wanted to touch it.

He pointed to the lettering surrounding the bucking horse. *Cody Nite Rodeo.* "We learn the name of the bareback champion in 1978, we identify our murder victim."

She turned the buckle over in her fingers.

Maybe things weren't so hopeless. Maybe they could still find a way out. Thanks to Eric. "And from there, we find out why he was killed."

Eric nodded. "And who killed him."

"You're thinking the sheriff did it?"

He shrugged a shoulder. "At the very least, he's trying to cover it up."

"So this whole thing…it's not about stolen money or drugs at all?"

"Maybe not." He gestured to the buckle in her hands. "Is there a list of the cowboys who've won awards like this? Something that goes back to 1978?"

"Pro rodeo results are listed on the PRCA Web site. But this is a year-end award for the Cody Nite Rodeo. I doubt there's a list online. Especially one that goes back to 1978." She searched her memory. She wasn't certain, but…

"What is it?"

"Back when I was barrel racing and Randy had just started riding bulls, I remember one place had the champions listed on the back of the grandstand. Like an honor role of sorts. I always dreamed of my name being up there someday."

"You think it was Cody?"

"I don't know, but Layton used to take Randy and me to the Cody rodeo pretty often."

"Then let's go to Cody."

"How? Walk? That should only take… forever."

"If we had to travel by road the whole way, that might be true. But as the crow flies…we aren't as far from Cody as you think."

Sarah scanned the topography. She'd gotten so turned around on their hike up to Saddle Horn Ridge and even more confused in their escape. "Where are we, exactly?"

He pointed to a narrow pass between two peaks. "Cody is that way, maybe thirty miles."

She looked down at his stocking foot. The bottom of his thick sock had worn away in spots, and the rusty color of dried blood colored the tattered edges. "Still a long way to walk."

"I'm betting we can find a ride." One corner of his mouth turned up.

She wanted to return the smile. Eric seemed as if he had thought the whole thing through, as if he had it all figured out. But while it felt good to have him with her, to be able to rely on him, to not have to handle everything herself, she knew things weren't so simple and clear-cut. And for all Eric's crooked smiles and confidence, she had the feeling he sensed that, too.

Chapter Nine

Although the brief stop for rest and water had helped, by the time they'd descended into the foothills, Sarah's bones ached with a fatigue from which she couldn't imagine recovering. Of course, Eric had it worse, traveling with only one boot. He hadn't said a word on the long hike down the mountain, but she'd been aware of his limp, which was growing more pronounced by the hour.

If they were where Eric said, they should find ranches and green hay fields flanking the river ahead. Civilization compared to the land they'd just crossed. Maybe there they could find the ride Eric had so cockily promised.

She sure hoped so, because she didn't know how he was going to manage to walk much farther.

The first ranch they came to seemed locked

up tight. No sign of life stirred in the house. The small barn, corral and fields were vacant, and the garage didn't have so much as a bicycle inside. "Must be a summer place," Eric said.

Sarah nodded. The beginning of June was summer in most places, but not necessarily here in the mountains. And even though the countryside was enjoying a nice growth spurt before the July sun dried the landscape to a dull brown, summer vacation and tourist season didn't really get cooking in this area until nearby Yellowstone opened its gates in a few weeks.

They moved on to the next ranch. Instead of hay fields, cattle dotted the valley. "Now we're talking," Eric said. "They must have some kind of vehicle."

"You're thinking of stealing a car?"

He nodded.

"Do you know how to do that?"

"I'm hoping I can figure it out."

She hoped so, too. And that the ranch didn't have dogs keeping watch. And that the rancher didn't have a gun. It seemed they were hanging a lot on hope. "There has to be a better way."

"You come up with one, I'm all ears."

They circled the house and crouched behind

a clump of big sage. From this angle, they had a clear view of the barn and other outbuildings. And in the middle of the gravel drive, a truck idled, hitched to a four-horse stock style trailer.

"I told you we'd find a ride. He even left the keys in and the engine running."

Movement stirred in the barn's open doorway.

"Wait." Sarah grabbed Eric's arm as if to stop him, even though he hadn't moved.

A dog trotted out, tail held high. Behind him, a man emerged leading a saddled horse. Lead rope loose in his hand, he stepped up into the trailer. The horse followed, horseshoes thunking on steel, as willing as if he was walking into his stall in the barn.

After a moment, the man jumped down from the back of the trailer. He closed the back gate and headed for the house, dog on his heels.

Clean Wranglers. Bright, striped button-down shirt. Perfectly shaped hat and a nice pair of boots. No cowboy dressed that well for day-to-day work. And although the saddle on the horse's back was no silver-encrusted monstrosity you sometimes saw in pleasure horse shows, it was as clean and spruced up as the man who would sit in it.

She glanced at the sun, hovering over the

mountains, poised to take a plunge. "You wanted to go to Cody? To the rodeo grounds?"

A smile turned both corners of Eric's lips. Two days worth of stubble shaded his chin. Evening sun slanted low through the sagebrush and sparkled in his green eyes. "I could kiss you."

A jitter lodged beneath her ribs.

"I mean, it's a good idea." He focused on the trailer.

She nodded. She knew that's what he meant. But somewhere dangerous inside her, she wanted it to be more.

LIKE EVERY PLACE IN Wyoming, it took much too long to drive to Cody, even though it was the closest town. Exhaust from the old truck swirled in the wind. Sarah's hair lashed against her cheeks. And the trailer's jolting motion actually made her grateful she hadn't eaten in a good number of hours. Even though they were sheltered behind a solid kick board rimming the lower half of the trailer, the wind felt more like a gale in October than a spring night in early June. By the time they reached town, it seemed Sarah couldn't do a thing to smooth the tangle on top of her head other than shave it off and start fresh.

The truck turned left and followed the light flow of traffic on the west strip, the road leading to the Buffalo Bill Dam and Yellowstone National Park. Sunset sparkled on the Shoshone River as the sun slipped behind the mountains. Hotels on the strip boasted few cars in their lots, the early tourist season trickle just a warm-up for the flood of people who would flock to enjoy the parks and a slice of the west come July.

The rodeo grounds loomed on the right, lights blazing. Tonight was rodeo night, as was every summer night in Cody. Even though she hadn't attended in years, some of her ranch hands... "Oh, no."

Eric's head whipped around. "What?"

"Keith and Glenn." She couldn't believe she hadn't thought of them. She only wished she was more aware of their plans. "They've been competing in team roping. They might be here tonight."

The truck turned in to the exhibitors' entrance and circled to the back of the arena.

Eric leveled a calm gaze. "If they see you, are they the types who will turn you in?"

She didn't have to think too hard about Glenn Freemont. "Glenn is. Between his fascination with crime novels and cop shows on television,

I suspect a career in law enforcement is his secret dream."

"And Keith?"

Keith Sherwood was another story. "Keith would probably prefer to shoot us himself." She supposed she should feel lucky that he didn't carry his assault rifle to rodeos, although she was sure he'd have an assortment of rifles in the rack in his truck along with a handgun or two.

"No loyalty, eh?"

"Glenn hasn't worked for me long. And I imagine Keith believes you killed Randy. He might even believe I was there, too, at this point." They had no clue how large the news story about the murder and subsequent manhunt had grown in the past day. Maybe the entire state would be gunning for them. And here they were, riding smack into the middle of a crowd of people, any one of whom could identify them, call the police, or worse. "This was a bad idea."

"It'll be fine. We'll be in and out before anyone sees us. We'll just have to avoid the competitors."

"Not such an easy thing to do when we're driving right into the middle of them."

They entered the gate and bumped through a

rutted lot between trucks, horse trailers and motor homes. Sarah peered through the slats in the back gate and focused on the small grandstand above the bucking chutes, a place called the Buzzard's Roost. Below were the stock pens. The scent of manure and the warm tang of horse sweat surrounded her like a favorite blanket. She took a deep, bracing breath. The trailer's jolts slowed as the truck circled.

Now came the tough part. Getting out of the trailer unseen. "Ready?"

Eric nodded. He rose to his feet, careful to stay tight to the side of the trailer in case anyone was behind them.

Sarah focused on his bloody sock. Another problem she'd forgotten about. "You might be a little noticeable walking around with only one boot."

"I have an idea." He motioned for her to move to the back gate. Once she took her spot, he placed his hands around her waist.

His touch felt familiar, comforting, but also disconcerting. Her body seemed to sway toward him on its own, leaning against the pressure of his hands, molding to his touch.

Stop it.

She focused on the slowing trailer, scouted

for stray riders warming up their mounts behind the trailer parking area. If anyone spotted them jumping from the trailer, they would be sure to ask questions. Questions she and Eric could never answer.

"As soon as your feet hit the ground, make for that rig over there." He extended a finger, indicating a motor home with a four-horse slant hitched to the back. "There shouldn't be anyone there. I just saw them leave."

"Okay. Ready." Sarah tensed. The trailer bumped, jolted and stopped.

Eric lifted her as if she weighed nothing. She grasped the trailer gate and swung her legs over. She hit the ground knees bent and running. The force shuddered through her bones.

She reached the other rig before the driver opened his pickup's door. Eric was right behind her, limping as fast as his fcct would move. They opened the trailer dressing room and ducked inside.

A dog's bark sounded from outside. A whistle split the air.

"Just in time." Sarah panted.

Eric checked out the tiny window in the dressing room's door. "All clear. No one seems to have noticed except the dog."

Sarah struggled to catch her breath. The rodeo had to be close to starting time. Likely most of the competitors had already drifted closer to the arena.

She glanced around the cramped and darkened space, the typical dressing room, tight and full of a jumbled form of organization that made sense only to the people to whom it belonged. She breathed in the warm fragrance of leather, mixed with Eric's distinctive scent.

He stepped to the side, his body pressing against her. "I found boot boxes. Yeah, these should do." He let out a soft grunt as he pulled one on.

She shifted to the side to give them both room. "How does it fit?"

"A little big on my good foot. But the other foot is so swollen, it's perfect."

"How about your head? I can still see some blood in your hair."

He added a black felt cowboy hat she found stuck in a corner and he was ready to go. "Don't you need something?"

"I'm fine," she said, although she didn't feel very fine at all. She glanced around the space. "Doesn't look like there's a woman that goes with this rig."

"Maybe we'll spot something on the way out."

She hated stealing peoples gear like this, especially since there was no way they could get it back to the poor guy when they were done. But it couldn't be helped. She didn't know how much cash Eric was carrying, but she didn't have a dime on her. When she'd gone out to do chores two evenings ago, she didn't exactly expect to need her wallet.

By the time they emerged from the dressing room, the man who'd acted as their unknowing chauffeur was nowhere to be seen. His dog barked from the rolled-down window of the pickup. Eric slung the backpack onto one shoulder. It didn't go with the outfit, but that couldn't be helped. They didn't exactly have a place to stash it. They strode through the exhibitors' area as if they belonged there.

A man in a silver belly Stetson and button-down shirt stood at the gate leading to the arena. "How the hell are we going to get around him?"

The sound of hooves trotting through gravel crunched behind them. Sarah glanced at Eric. "Slow down, I have an idea."

A tiny boy bounced past them on the back of a towering quarter horse, well over sixteen hands. Sarah plastered a proud-parent smile on her face and followed the boy through the gate as if he belonged to her.

The man in the hat gave the kid a grin, then focused on Sarah and Eric. "Good luck," he called.

"Thanks!" Sarah said.

Eric gave the guy a friendly tip of the hat. As soon as they cleared the gate, he turned to Sarah. "Pretty slick."

She couldn't help turning a genuine smile on him. In the past day and a half, she'd had to lean on Eric more than she had leaned on anyone since she was a child. It felt good to have a venue where she could put her expertise to use. And it felt better than she wanted to acknowledge to have Eric notice. "I'm glad he didn't know the boy. That would have been dicey."

"You'd have come up with something."

She'd like to think so, but she wasn't so sure. Her mind felt as fuzzy as her muscles were tired. Along with the fatigue, she couldn't shake the constant sense that tears were pressing at the corners of her eyes and longing poised to uncurl in her chest—emotion waiting for the slightest excuse to push to the surface. She normally went by what her gut told her, but fighting through all she had in addition to having Eric again at her side was overwhelming. She prayed she could hold it all together.

And that they wouldn't run in to Keith or Glenn or someone else who would know who they were.

Finding the track that circled the opposite end of the arena from where the competitors congregated, they headed for the grandstand. They fell into the light stream of foot traffic behind a young family. Sarah plastered a smile to her face and tried to look like she was here to enjoy a fun night at the rodeo instead of hoping to identify a murder victim.

In front of her, a toddler girl looked over her daddy's shoulder and gave her a smile. Wrapping her little arms around his neck, she whispered something in his ear, and he laughed. Her older brother held both mom and dad's hands. Picking up his legs, he swung between them like they were human monkey bars.

Sarah's throat felt thick, her chest painfully empty. What she wouldn't have given for a happy family scene like that when she was a child. Her parents rarely took them to the rodeo, only Layton had bothered to do that. Even when one of them did trailer her barrel horse to the grounds, usually their mom, she seemed distant, more inclined to hang out with adults than help her daughter or cheer for her son to stay on his steer for the required eight seconds.

The worst part was that Sarah had always vowed her kids would have it different. That their rodeo experiences would be all about family. A mom and a dad…together. A mom and a dad who loved each other. She'd always wished she could give her own children those moments she'd never had. Precious moments the family in front of them probably took for granted.

She blinked back the mist of tears and gave the little girl a wave as the family split off to take a seat in the stands and she and Eric continued on the same path.

In the concession area behind the grandstand, people milled around, buying raffle tickets to win a bedroom set handcrafted out of knotty pine. The crowd seemed bigger than the parking lot suggested. The scent of popcorn teased the air, making Sarah's stomach growl. She looked up at the back of the grandstand.

Plain, white walls greeted her, broken only by a few sponsors signs.

Her stomach dropped. "It's not here. The list of champions."

From the arena, the announcer boomed his introductions. Boots shuffled in the stands above them. Flags flapped in the wind as riders paraded them around the arena at a lope.

"There are seats on the other side," Eric said. "Maybe it's there."

Sarah thought of the small section of grandstand overlooking the bucking chutes, where cowboys mounted horses and bulls, and shook her head. "I got a glimpse of The Buzzard's Roost when we pulled in. It wasn't there either. I must be remembering the wall of champions from a different rodeo grounds. I have so many memories of this place, I guess I just assumed…"

Eric rubbed a hand over her back. "It's okay. We'll find his name another way."

His touch felt good, as it had in the trailer. Too good. She wanted to lean in to him. Let him hold her. Fill her up. She felt too weak to stand on her own a moment longer.

She shook her head and beat back the threat of tears. She supposed it was natural to have this reaction. Between the hormones and lack of sleep and losing her brother, it probably wasn't surprising that she was now losing her mind. "We came here for nothing."

"Pardon, but don't I know you?" a man's voice called from behind her.

Sarah's heart stuttered in her chest.

Chapter Ten

Eric's pulse thrummed in his ears, drowning out the first strains of the national anthem. He glanced at the front gate. A good fifty feet lay between them and the parking lot. If this guy recognized them, they'd have to make a dash for it. Gathering himself, he turned toward the voice.

An older man stood grinning at Sarah, his face as round as the brim of the hat on his head. He raised a hand and stroked the corners of a nearly white mustache. "Didn't you used to do some barrel racing around here a few years ago?"

Sarah glanced at Eric with wide eyes, then returned her focus to the man. Pink crept up her throat and touched her cheeks. She opened her mouth, as if to answer, then closed it without saying a word.

Eric thrust his had toward the man. "I'm Joe.

So you've been involved with the rodeo here for a while?" He'd learned a while ago that if you wanted to distract someone, get them talking about themselves. It worked every time.

The man enveloped his hand and gave it a firm shake. "They call me Smithy. Been coming here since I was a boy up in Powell."

"Then you're just the man we want to talk to, Smithy." He knew it was risky, sticking around any longer than they had to. The guy's memory could come back at any moment. And if he re-membered Sarah's name, he might just tie her to the story he'd heard about in the news. But without the list of champions, they were without answers…answers Smithy just might be able to provide.

He had to take the risk.

Eric pulled the belt buckle from the pack. "We came upon this out on the BLM. Wanted to return it to its owner. Problem is, we don't know the name of the man who won it."

The man took the buckle and held it out as far as he could reach. Hard muscle roped forearms spotted with age. "Bareback bronc riding?"

"1978." Eric supplied.

"Long time ago."

Sarah gave him a smile, this time looking

more sweet than scared out of her wits. "Are there records of who won back then?"

"Of course."

"Where could we find something like that?" Her voice was still a little shaky, but curious. She'd obviously recovered from the shock and was playing along nicely. As if they'd planned this course of action all along.

She never ceased to amaze him.

The man stroked his mustache once again, then trailed lower to rub his chin between fingers and thumb. "1978...I think I can tell you who won this. But if you want to check—"

"Really? Who?" Sarah jumped in a little too quickly.

Smithy narrowed his eyes on her as if once again trying to remember where he'd seen her before.

"We just need to get back to our children." Eric motioned to the stands. The lie had slipped out so easily, and it suddenly struck him that in just a few months, it wouldn't be a lie any longer. "You understand."

Smithy smiled. "Rodeo's fun for a family." He motioned to the arena and began telling them about an upcoming event where children in the audience tried to capture a ribbon from a calf's tail and win prizes.

Eric didn't hear a word.

A family. That's what he and Sarah and the baby could be. His throat constricted. He kept his focus on Smithy, smiling and nodding at the older man's story, careful not to look in Sarah's direction, careful to keep control of the emotion bubbling inside.

He'd never wanted a family. Never considered it. He told himself he liked his life as it was. Clear-cut and logical. Always in control. Being around Sarah was never that. He always felt like he was over his head, scaling a cliff solo with no harness. Just a slip away from a disastrous fall.

But right now, listening to Smithy, thinking about a life with her, a family with her...

"So if you'd like me to look up the winner of that buckle to be official..."

Eric forced his mind back to the conversation at hand. Before he had time to think about any of that, he needed to make sure Sarah was safe. And the way to do that was to get some answers.

"Do you know who it belongs to? Off the top of your head?" he prompted. "We don't need anything official."

Smithy handed the buckle back to Eric. "Larry Hodgeson's the one you're looking for."

"You're sure?" The man had come up with the name so easily, Eric was almost afraid to believe him.

"Sure, I'm sure. He beat me out for that buckle. I can still feel that last ride on rainy days." He rubbed his hip to illustrate. "A man don't forget something like that."

"Thank you so much." This was turning out better than Eric had dreamed. "Do you know where he lives?"

"Cheyenne. At least last I heard, that's where he was. Worked for the state down there, I believe."

Eric almost groaned. The capital of Wyoming, Cheyenne was in the opposite corner of the state from Cody. He didn't relish the thought of that drive. Of course, driving wasn't even possible unless they located some wheels.

"You want to return that buckle, you can give it to me. I'll give it to his wife. She lives here in Cody."

"His wife?" Sarah echoed.

"Ex-wife, I should have said. After they divorced a little while back, Joy moved home.

She's got family here, you know. She can probably make sure it gets back to him."

"If you don't mind, we'd like to return the buckle to Joy ourselves. I'd love to meet her." Sarah gave the man a smile that could charm just about any man out of anything. "Do you know where we can find her?" she asked.

Once again the man studied her with narrowed eyes. "I ain't in the habit of giving out ladies' addresses to strangers."

"Maybe she would meet us somewhere?" Eric asked. It was up to Eric to get the man's attention away from Sarah and focused on him. Smithy obviously still felt he should know her, and judging from his expressions every time she spoke, he wasn't about to give up until her remembered her name.

Sarah shifted her boots on the gravel under her feet. "If you think she's too busy, that's all right."

"Too busy?" The man shook his head so hard his jowls flapped. "Joy would welcome a social call. Let me ask her. What section are you and the kids sitting in?"

"What section?" Sarah glanced at Eric.

To the man, it probably looked like she just couldn't recall. Eric knew she was feeling the same jolt at being caught in a lie that rattled through his own stomach. But there was more implied in the man's comment than a question they couldn't answer. He grasped her hand and gave it a reassuring squeeze. "Is Joy Hodgeson here at the rodeo?" he asked.

"She don't miss a night. She's up in the announcer's booth. Acts as kind of a secretary up there, keeping track of the entrants and such." He pointed to the announcer's booth across the arena in the top of the Buzzard's Roost. "One of the reasons she moved back, I think. They have a grand rodeo in Cheyenne, but it ain't Cody."

Sarah nodded. "Good memories. I can appreciate that. I'd love to meet her. Is there any way we can pop in to talk to her? It'll only take a second, and I've always wanted to see what everything looks like from up there."

Those narrowed eyes again. "I knew you were from around here."

Eric sucked in a breath. He groped for a distraction. Something he could say. A question he could ask. A way to take back control of the situation. This time, he came up empty.

"You know how people say they never forget a face? That's me. At least my wife swears it." He looked at her as if waiting for her to fess up.

This time, Sarah gave him a relaxed smile that

should have had her up for some kind of acting award. "I ran the barrels when I was a teenager. I have a lot of good memories of this place as well. I'd love to talk to Mrs. Hodgeson."

"Can I tell her your name?"

There it was. Eric hoped she could come up with something. Because even if Mr. Never-forget-a-face didn't recognize them from photos on TV, he might have heard their names enough over the past two days that it all would click into place.

"Mary Ann Johnston was my maiden name. I didn't win much, so I doubt you'd remember. I sure had a good time, though." Emotion infused her voice—too much real feeling for anyone to fake.

Eric almost did a double take.

"Mary Ann…Mary Ann…you've grown up a lot, young lady. And here I was thinking you looked like that Trask girl. Well, follow me, Joe and Mary Ann." He started walking back around the track that curved the arena's edge, motioning them to follow with a wave of his arm.

Sarah glanced at Eric, relief plain on her face.

Eric seconded that feeling. He didn't know how she'd come up with the name, but it had worked. He'd been caught flat-footed that time, and she'd pulled it out. The feeling that someone had his back, so to speak, that if he faltered she'd step in, was a new experience, one he didn't entirely know how to process.

Eric and Sarah followed the man up a steel staircase and onto a walkway. A day and a half had passed since Randy had been shot, but it seemed like they'd been on the run without sleep for a week. The setting sun glowed orange off the Absarokas to the west, its reflection making the Shoshone River look as if it were on fire. Below, horses, steers and bulls milled in steel-pipe pens, waiting for their turn in the arena. The announcer's voice boomed out the name of the first bareback rider on the program, and a roar went up from the crowd.

They had one more person to talk to. One more role to play, and hopefully they'd get the answers they needed. He just prayed at least one of them was still sharp enough to get the job done.

JOY HODGESON WASN'T anything like what Sarah had imagined. Shockingly white hair cropped short and stylish and dressed in Wranglers and a form-fitting western shirt with hot pink piping, the woman looked far younger than she had to be. And her energy…the way she was flying around, organizing entry forms, and feeding them to the announcer, made Sarah feel even more tired than she already was.

After making introductions, Smithy stepped to the side of the narrow staircase outside the booth's door. "Go on in. There's not enough room in there for me, too. Besides, that place gives me claustrophobia *and* vertigo. It's like a damn tree house without the tree."

Eric motioned for Sarah to go first and the two of them crammed in to the little room. The place smelled of new paint and cigarettes. Smithy closed the door behind them. The announcer didn't even turn around, his ball cap pulled down to his brows, his attention glued to the action in the arena below.

"So what brings you two up to see me?" Joy managed to beam them a friendly smile at the same time as she organized entry forms for the next event and handed them to the announcer. Down in the arena, a man dressed as a ragged clown launched into a comedy routine.

"We have something you might want to take a look at." Eric pulled out the belt buckle and handed it to the woman.

She stared at the tarnished silver and ran a fingertip over its gold lettering.

"Smithy said it might have belonged to your husband?" Sarah prodded.

"Yep. It's Larry's. Where did you get it?"

Sarah glanced at Eric, but she didn't have to look to him to know the last thing either one of them wanted to do was give Joy a truthful answer to that question. "We found it out on the BLM."

"Careless fool." She handed it back to Eric. "It's nice of you to return it, don't get me wrong. I just…I've put that part of my life behind me. If you give me your name and number, I'll have him call you if he ever comes looking for it."

"When was the last time you saw your husband?"

"Oh, I threw him out over two years ago."

Sarah didn't have to spend much time counting the months to know the body in the crevasse probably hadn't been there that long. She was no forensics expert, but she'd assume the bones would be clean and the smell gone after that amount of time in the elements. And the smell had definitely not been gone. "Smithy said you moved back to Cody not long ago. That you used to live in Cheyenne."

The woman bobbed her head as she laid out the entrants on the table in front of the announcer.

The man focused on his job, still not taking the time to spare them so much as a glance.

"I love Cheyenne, don't get me wrong. But I only moved there because of Larry's job. Cody is my home."

"Where does Larry work?" Eric managed to make the question sound natural, as if they were merely having a casual conversation.

She waved her hands in front of her as if erasing words from the air. "He doesn't work there anymore. Not long after our divorce, he up and quit his job. Here he just had to stay in Cheyenne instead of moving back with me, and yet he didn't even wait to take advantage of the incentives for early retirement." She shook her head and clucked her tongue as if the illogic of it still bothered her.

"What did he do for a living?" Sarah asked.

"Oh, he worked for the state. In the crime lab."

"The crime lab?" She exchanged a look with Eric. "What did he do there?"

"He looked at fingerprints. It was a good job. But sometimes I wish I'd never encouraged him to go back to school. I wish we'd stayed right here and worked my folks' ranch."

Sarah tilted her head. "Why is that? It seems like a pretty good job."

"It was. Not great money, but steady, good hours and health insurance. But that was before all those shows started on TV. You know, *CSI* and the like."

Now Sarah wasn't following her at all. "What about *CSI?*"

"Nothing against the show, but Larry started thinking he was one of those TV stars or something. He started talking with a writer. Having lunch." She made air quotes with her fingers around the word *lunch.* "Getting a bit of a swelled head, I think. That's when I left. He didn't even try to talk me out of it. Probably had visions of dating some television star in a low-cut blouse."

A knock sounded on the door. Joy scootched past them and opened the door a crack. A man pushed a file of entries into Joy's hand.

Eric pulled the brim of his hat down to shield his features and Sarah turned her face to the side. She gazed over the announcer's shoulder, pretending to be studying a skit that two clowns—or bullfighters, as they liked to be called—performed to kill time while the announcer and Joy and all the people running things behind the scenes readied the next event's entries. Best to be safe. There was always a chance whomever was at the door was more of a news hound than either Joy or Smithy.

The door thunked closed, and Sarah let out a heavy breath of relief.

Joy wedged herself through the tight space once again. "I got the breakaway roping here next, Billy."

"All right." The announcer turned, hand reaching for the file. He looked up at Eric… and froze.

Sarah's blood froze with him.

Seemingly in slow motion, he reached for the microphone. He turned on the switch and leaned his lips close. *"Security. I need security. Up here in the announcer's booth. Hurry."*

Chapter Eleven

Eric grabbed Sarah's arm, but he didn't need to. She was already moving, throwing open the door, racing down the steel steps. They reached the main walkway and dashed past a concession stand. Their feet thundered on the steel grating.

Two men in Stetsons rounded the corner. Shoulder to shoulder, they nearly blocked the stairs.

Sarah slammed to a stop, Eric almost running in to her from behind. She whirled around, looked up at him, the whites of her eyes bright in the arena lights.

He had to get her out of here. He had to think.

The men started up the steps in unison, a wall of cowboy they couldn't get around. Eric spun in the other direction. A man came at them from that direction, too. Striding out from the seats of The Buzzard's Roost. Another entered the walkway behind him.

Eric had to do something *now*.

He grabbed the rail and looked over the edge. A maze of steel fence shown in the dimness, ten or fifteen feet below, chutes that returned bucking horses and bulls to the holding pens. He grabbed Sarah's arm. "Over the edge."

She nodded, no hesitation. Grabbing the rail, she swung a leg over the edge and jumped.

Eric followed. He hit the ground behind her. The impact sent a stab of pain through his foot and a shudder through his body. But the ground was soft, stirred up by hooves and padded with manure.

"Eric!" On her feet already, Sarah was moving for the gate. He struggled to his feet and followed.

Voices clamored behind them. The tramping of feet rumbled down the stairs.

Sarah half climbed, half vaulted one pipe gate, then another. She slipped over the last of the gates designed to funnel the bucking stock and disappeared into a holding pen.

Eric followed her path. Each time he jumped a gate and landed, his foot screamed. By the third one, his foot was numb.

Fine by him.

He raced across the churned-up ground of the pen. A loud snort sounded to his right. He glanced in the direction of the sound. A huge gray bull stared back.

Damn.

"Over here. Just run for it."

He made for the sound of Sarah's voice. Behind him, he could hear the animal. The beat of his hooves. The snort of his breath. He braced himself for goring horns.

Sarah stood near the fence. She flapped something in her hands, something…

The bull raced straight for her.

"No." Eric veered to the side.

"Keep running! Jump the fence!" she yelled.

Her coat. That's what she held. She waved it like she thought she was some damn Spanish bullfighter. As the bull drew close, she tossed it. It fluttered in the air. He stabbed into it with his horns and dashed it to the ground.

Sarah jumped for the fence. Ten feet down, Eric did, too. They clambered over. When their feet hit the ground on the other side, they raced for the back gate.

Men's voices jangled behind them. Asking questions. Yelling directions. Someone shouted he'd called police.

Eric pushed his legs to move faster. When they'd arrived, a man in a cowboy hat had been watching the gate. No one was there now. Eric could only guess that he'd responded to the call for security. That he was one of the men pursuing them now.

Eric grasped the chain looped around the gate's latch. He yanked it open and he and Sarah slipped through. He veered to the left, racing past the trailers and motor homes.

Sarah motioned to the jumble of rigs. "We—"

"Too obvious." No way they could stow away aboard a random trailer now. Not with men combing the grounds for them, men who would be out of the stands and smack on their trail at any moment. It was the first place they'd look. "The river."

They ran across the flat area as fast as they could, gravel shifting and scattering under their feet like marbles. The gravel ended and the ground grew rough. When they hit the spot where it started sloping down to the river, Eric dove for the dirt, pulling Sarah with him.

Behind them, shouting came closer, rising over the sound of the river's rushing water. Eric scooped in breath after breath, trying to satisfy his hungry lungs. The faint odor of sulfur in the water hung in the back of this throat. "We'll follow the river bed to the highway. We have to get out of here before the police arrive."

Cheeks pink from their escape, Sarah nodded. Her eyes glowed with determination. Her dark hair swirled around her in the wind. She looked so alive and vibrant, his chest hurt.

He had to get her out of this mess. He had to find someplace safe. He looked at the rushing water. "Ready?"

Sarah nodded. "I'm right behind you."

He jammed the black hat low to cover as much of his hair as he could and half crawled, half stumbled down the bank to the water, keeping his body as low to the ground as he could. Rock bit into his hands, his knees. He kept moving, Sarah right behind him.

Above the roar of the water and thunder of his pulse, voices rose in the night air. Somewhere a siren screamed.

They had no time to lose.

SARAH COULDN'T REMEMBER ever being so cold.

They followed the river until it flanked the highway. Most of the way, they were able to stay on the shore. But in some spots, the bank rose almost vertically from the water. Then, they had to plunge into the frigid river. Deeper than the stream that crossed through her ranch, the Shoshone's current tumbled and swirled around them, fast and relentless. And even though she was soaked and scared and drained of any energy she had left, she was grateful to make it to the highway alive and not in the custody of police.

They followed West Yellowstone Avenue, and turned toward downtown. They needed to find a car or a place to hide, and the other direction only promised the reservoir and a road that dead-ended at the closed gates of Yellowstone. But still, walking into civilization made Sarah nervous.

She tried not to look behind her. Tried not to focus on the red and blue lights pulsing from the rodeo grounds. There wasn't a lot of foot traffic in this stretch of Cody, making it hard to blend in. So they stayed off the highway, moving through ditches and along parking lots.

Eric reached out a hand to help her up a steep ditch and to a more level cluster of driveways leading to restaurants and motels, busy on a Saturday night. "You're trembling. Cold?"

She nodded. But that wasn't the half of it. The cold, the fear, the ebbing adrenaline…her list went on. But try as she might, she couldn't stop shaking. It wasn't within her grasp. Not any longer. The best she could do was stumble forward and pray Eric was in better shape.

He rubbed a hand over her back as they walked. "So if you were a tourist, where would you want to stay?"

She glanced at him out of the corner of her eye.

"Come on. Price is no object." He gave her a smile that seemed a little tired and forced, but she had to admit it was better than she could have done.

She could at least put in what effort she could muster. "The Irma," she said, suggesting the famous hotel Buffalo Bill Cody named for his daughter.

"A sucker for history, eh?"

"You bet."

A police car sped past, lights flashing red and blue.

Sarah sucked in a breath and tried her best to keep focused straight ahead, to look like she didn't have a care in the world, not that she remembered what that felt like anymore.

"What would you have for dinner?"

She forced her mind back to Eric's game. "A steak, of course. Baked potato with sour cream.

A salad, ranch dressing." Her stomach growled, right on cue.

"Steak, huh? Who would have guessed? I suppose a beef rancher is required to say that."

"Hey, it's real food, that's what Layton always likes to say. How about you? You're not going to choose seafood or quiche or something, are you?"

He didn't answer. His steps slowed.

"What is it?"

"Not sure."

They cleared the strip mall and walked to the next drive. A small restaurant sat off on its own at the back of the parking lot, a sign in front proclaiming it had the best steaks in town. The building was cute but older, built of rough-hewn logs and sporting a green roof that made Sarah think of kids' Lincoln Logs. But unlike the restaurants they'd passed earlier, the lot in front was vacant and no lights shone from the interior.

Eric pointed to a sign on the front door announcing the restaurant was temporarily closed for renovation. "I can't promise a room at the Irma, but I might be able to get you that steak."

ERIC CARRIED A BUCKET of fried chicken the workers must have had left over from lunch and plopped it on the table. He added two dinner plates and linen napkins he'd found in the waiter's aisle.

"You promised me steak," she said, lighting a candle with a wooden match. Gentle light flickered over the booth.

Covered with thick upholstered padding and wide enough for sleeping, the booths were the first thing Eric had spotted after they broke in through a window that was fortunately not alarmed. In addition, the pantry and walk-in freezer still held a stock of staples and the plumbing in the kitchen worked like a dream. They would even have coffee in the morning.

Eric set down two tall glasses of water and slid into the opposite bench. "Have I ever told you that you're awfully picky?"

"Funny, I've always thought I wasn't picky enough." She tilted her head to the side and gave him a smile.

For a moment, he felt like they'd turned back time. That he'd never walked away from her. That no one had been killed. That the police and sheriff and half the state of Wyoming weren't looking for them now. That all he had to concentrate on was how good being around her made him feel. To accept it. To soak it in.

It was a nice fantasy.

For a long while, all they did was eat and drink, not wasting even a moment on talk. By the time they came up for air, the bucket of chicken was empty and piles of bones lay on the plates.

Sarah tilted the bucket toward her and picked crumbs of greasy breading from the bottom. "Hope the workers bring a lunch tomorrow. This 'being fugitives' stuff has turned us into criminals."

"We could always leave them some cash to pay for it."

"How much cash do you have?"

"Under fifty dollars. Forty-eight to be exact."

Her smile faded. Clearly she understood there was no way they could get more. Not without the law tracking them down. "I guess they'll just have to deal with it."

Eric was sorry he'd brought it up. For a moment, they'd had a little reprieve, food, relative safety…they'd been able to forget a little. He was sorry his comment had brought them crashing back to earth. "Ready for dessert?" The lightness in his voice sounded forced, even to his own ears.

She arched her brows. "Dessert?"

Eric thrust himself up from the booth and

strode into the bar area. Even in the dim light, he could make out boxes lining the wall. What he wouldn't give for a stiff shot of whiskey. But since Sarah couldn't drink because of her pregnancy, he skipped over the booze boxes and found a different kind of treat. Twisting open the jar's cap, he carried it back to the table and set it in front of Sarah.

"Maraschino cherries?" A chuckle escaped from her throat. "I haven't had these since I was a kid with a love for hot fudge sundaes."

"I'm afraid that's the only part of the sundae I can manage." Although he'd found some staples like sealed, premeasured bags of coffee that were still stored in back, steak and ice cream and other perishables were harder to find in a restaurant closed for renovation.

She plucked out a cherry by the stem and took it between her teeth. Tearing it from the stem, she closed her eyes as if it was the most decadent of treats. She opened her eyes. "Aren't you going to have one?"

"Maybe I'll just watch."

Her laugh sounded deep and rich and intimate, and he realized it had been a long time since he'd heard it. "Feeling better?" he asked.

"Trying. I think my mind needed food."

He was sure she needed sleep, too. Probably more than they could afford to take. But if she was like him, her mind churning these questions would make sleep unlikely. At least until they decided what they were going to do next. "At least we came up with a name for our murdered man."

The candle's flicker caused shadows to shift across Sarah's face. "I kept finding myself wanting to tell Joy her husband was dead. It's sad that she thinks he grew too arrogant to talk to her."

"There are a lot of things that are sad about this mess." He'd lost count.

"A lot that's confusing, too. I can't figure out why on earth a sheriff would want to kill a fingerprint analyst."

Eric felt relieved to focus on the mystery at hand. Mistakes and motives of other people were a lot easier to examine than his own. "Because Hodgeson wouldn't give him the result he wanted?"

"But his wife said he was retired. Has been for a while. So he wouldn't be working on any pending cases. Maybe it was personal?"

He tilted his head to the side, considering. Could a sheriff in Norris County and a state crime lab analyst in Cheyenne have a personal connection? It was possible. Of course, knowing as little as they knew, a lot of things were possible. "Or Larry Hodgeson found evidence in an old case, something Sheriff Gillette wants buried."

"What kind of evidence? Fingerprints they hadn't noticed before?"

He shrugged a shoulder. "I'm just grasping at straws. But we'll find out."

"How?"

It was a good question. They'd gotten a break in finding this restaurant tonight. They needed another. "Tomorrow we check out junkyards, car lots, whatever. See if we can find a vehicle that runs."

"Steal one, you mean."

There was nothing he could do about that. "I doubt forty-eight bucks will buy one."

"And then?"

"We need to find out more about Larry Hodgeson. If we know who he was, what he worked on, maybe we can come up with why someone would want him dead."

She nodded. "But how do we do that? That's what I can't figure out. We can't very well drive down to Cheyenne and waltz into the crime lab. Seems a bit bold."

He gave her a teasing grin. "You've got to admit, Sheriff Gillette wouldn't expect it."

"Right," she said, tone dry as the Bighorn Basin in August.

"Actually I was thinking of newspapers."

Sarah nodded. "The writer. Joy said he was talking to a writer."

"Exactly."

"We can search for news stories mentioning him online. The library has computers we can use."

"Still risky." He still felt shaken by their close call at the rodeo grounds. Even now the police could be tracking them down. Closing in on the restaurant under the cover of darkness.

He watched Sarah pop another cherry into her mouth. Whenever he looked at her, touched her, heard the sound of her voice, a need to protect her welled up inside him like a snow-melt flood.

He'd always felt too much for her, and the past two days, those feelings had grown tenfold. The threat of something going wrong, her getting hurt, something happening to the baby...all of it was hard to take. And the hardest thing to accept was that he had so little control over what happened next. From the moment

Randy had been shot and the sheriff had shown up at Sarah's ranch, he had been scrambling to react, to keep disaster from crashing down on them and sweeping them away. So far, he'd barely been half a step ahead.

"What is it?" Sarah leaned forward, hands splayed on the table in front of her.

He forced himself to take a deep breath. "Nothing. I just…the risk can't be helped. But we'll find a library in some other town. They'll have their eyes out for us here in Cody." He looked down at her hands.

Her fingers were trembling. She folded her hands together. "Okay."

For all their attempts at lightness and conversation, they were both exhausted. It was amazing they were still holding it together as well as they were. "We'll find answers, Sarah. I promise."

"That's a promise you might not be able to keep."

Maybe not. But at least he could try. He could give it everything he had.

He fitted his hands over hers and gave them a gentle squeeze. Her fingers felt so fine in his big mitt, so delicate. Yet he'd seen her use those hands to rope cattle and string fence right along with the men who worked for her. She was strong. But even strong people had vulnerabilities. Even strong people needed to be able to rely on someone.

A tremble centered deep in his chest. Had he been afraid of being that someone? Was that why he left just as things between them were getting serious? Was that what caused the jumble of emotion inside him whenever she was near?

He wasn't sure. But there was one thing he did know. Now that Sarah was in danger, now that they had a baby on the way, he no longer had the right to opt out. Scared, confused, none of that mattered. He had to be that someone Sarah could rely on. And he couldn't let anything get in the way.

Chapter Twelve

Sarah soaked in the feel of Eric's hands sheltering hers and watched the candle's flicker play across his face. Over the months since he'd told her he couldn't see her anymore, the months the life they'd created was growing inside her, she'd longed for moments like this. His eyes looking at her as if she was the most fascinating thing he'd ever seen. His skin touching hers. His voice washing over her, full of feeling he didn't often show. She wanted to believe all of it was real. Lasting. Not merely the by-product of their situation.

Unfortunately, she was far too pragmatic for that. "I have to know something. Something kind of off-topic."

His brows lowered. "Yeah?"

Pressure squeezed at the base of her throat and hollowed out her chest. It was one thing feeling this insecurity about Eric, wondering about him deep in the back of her mind. It was another to broach the subject out loud. But after their trek through the mountains, the way her body wanted to sway into him at every touch, the way she longed for him to fold her into his arms, the need she had to kiss him…she had to know the truth. "Why did you leave? Three months ago, why did you walk away?"

He tilted his head, shadows sinking around his eyes, making them unreadable. "I used to think I knew the answer to that."

"I remember what you told me. Every single word. That a man who climbed mountains for a living couldn't commit to a serious relationship. That you were doing it for me, to protect me from future heartbreak. It just never made a lot of sense to me. It seemed like an excuse."

He rolled his lips inward, pausing before he spoke. "I suppose it was."

She leaned against the back of the bench. She felt empty, exhausted. Too tired to speak. Too tired to think. As if the fatigue she'd been struggling to hold off had swamped her. "I wish you hadn't bothered with excuses. I wish you had just told me the truth outright. It would have been easier for me that way."

His brows dipped low. He shook his head a little from side to side. "What do you think the truth is?"

It seemed obvious. "That you didn't care for me enough. Not enough to stay, to have a future."

"That's not it."

"Then what is it?"

"I'm just…I'm not good at this kind of thing. I'm just not—"

"Give me a break." She wished at that moment she hadn't brought any of it up. "The last thing I want is more excuses."

"What do you want?"

"The truth."

"The truth." He stared at the cherry jar, as if convinced the truth was hiding between the little artificially red orbs. "I'm not sure what the truth is, but I can tell you how I felt. How I feel even now."

Inwardly, she braced herself. "So tell me."

"I had this sense that something was bound to go wrong. That I was losing control. Just this general sense of dread."

"Dread? Of what?"

He shook his head. "I'm not sure. It was like…it was like the way I felt after my father died."

She remembered the story, at least the facts. He'd died in a car accident when Eric was fourteen. One day he'd climbed off the school bus to find police officers in the living room and his mother sobbing. But while Eric had told her the facts, he'd never talked about the emotions he'd gone through. Eric had rarely talked about emotions at all. But she knew him, the things he liked. The things he couldn't stand. She remembered. "You felt out of control?"

He let out a heavy sigh. "My mom cried herself to sleep every night. I heard her through the walls. And there was more. She took pills. Drank. I watched her self-destruct right in front of me, like the grief was grinding down what was left of her."

"That must have been horrible." She ached for him, for the boy he'd been. She ached for his mother, a woman she'd never met.

"One moment my life was secure and logical, the next…it was like everything I knew had been blown away."

She'd like to say she understood, that she knew the feeling. But the truth was, except for the ranch land itself and perhaps Layton, her life had been anything but secure and logical. Her parents' marriage, the worries about what

Randy would do next…all of that seemed subject to a cruel whim.

Of course, maybe that just made her better at adapting. "So you were worried about things changing? And that's why you left?"

"Change? No." Muscles drew tight around his mouth, his forehead. He looked as if he was in pain. As if the dread he talked about in the past was here. Rooted in her.

"Then what is it?"

"The feelings. The lack of control. I just…it scared me."

It seemed ludicrous. Here was this big, strong man, a man who scaled mountains, and he was talking about being afraid. "What scared you? Me?"

"No, me." He held up a hand. "I know it sounds stupid. Right now, I can hardly believe I let those words out of my mouth. But it's the truth. When I met you, I wasn't looking to get married. You're right about that. I wasn't expecting to feel as much for you as I did. It just all seemed too fast. Crazy."

"Out of control."

"Yeah. I needed to get away and think. I could never really think when I was around you." He rubbed his forehead with thumb and forefinger. "I still can't."

That, she understood. The fire between them had burned fast and furious from the beginning. The difference was, she could never manage to pull herself away. She never wanted to. "And now that you've been away? Now that you've had a chance to think?"

"I've asked you to marry me."

"Because I'm pregnant."

"Not just that." He leaned forward on his elbows and took her hands, one in each of his own. "I won't leave you again, Sarah. I can promise you that. I will never again let you down."

Tears misted Sarah's eyes, turning the dim dining room into a mosaic of shadow and light. She didn't know how she could possibly have more tears to cry, but here they were.

Three months ago, she'd yearned to hear those words from Eric. That commitment. That promise. Now she wasn't sure what to think. But there was one thing she no longer had questions about. "I know you'll come through for me, Eric."

The ridges lining his forehead seemed to smooth in the flickering light.

She had the sudden urge to kiss him. To lean in and take his face in her hands. To fit her lips to his mouth. To taste him and hold him and never let him go.

She clamped her bottom lip between her teeth.

He drew in a breath and focused on a spot above her head. When he returned his gaze to hers, his eyes glistened. "I hope you reconsider my offer. Once you've had a chance to think about it, I mean. Once all this is finished."

She looked away from him and concentrated on the candle's flame. "Our baby will be lucky to have you for a father." She wanted to see his expression, but didn't dare meet his eyes. One look and she could change her mind. One kiss and she'd be a goner. She had to hold fast.

He shifted on the bench. "But?"

"But you don't love me."

"You don't know how I feel."

"Neither do you." She brought her eyes to his despite the risk. She saw something there. Affection, certainly. Caring. Always desire. But love? She didn't know what that would look like.

He reached across the table and took her hand back into his. "What if I told you I think I'm falling?"

She shook her head.

"What do I need to do? Make me understand. What do you want?"

"I—I want you to be different."

"Different?"

"Stupid, huh?" She let out a stab of laughter. It echoed through the room, stiff and inappropriate.

He didn't say anything. He obviously didn't know what to say.

She couldn't blame him. But the fact was, he didn't need to speak. She did. He just needed to listen. "I won't have an empty marriage like my parents did. I want a man who loves me. I've always promised myself that, and I won't give it up. Even for you."

"I don't want you to give that up."

"No?"

"I just want you to give me a chance."

She pressed her fingers to closed eyelids until color exploded in plumes and swirls. She wanted to. She wanted him. Enough to make excuses of her own, rationalizations just to be with him, to believe he loved her like she deserved. Like she needed. And that he always would.

"I'm sorry, Eric." She shook her head. "I can't do that."

ERIC JOLTED OFF THE bench. For a moment, he didn't know where he was. Dark shapes loomed to either side. The odor of paint and newly laid tile hung in the air. Outside, a truck roared past.

His heart pounded against his ribs. He gasped air as if he'd been running for his life in his dreams.

Was that what had awakened him? A dream?

He knew instinctively he'd been asleep for only a few hours, and those hours had been anything but restful. All he remembered was the feeling of chaos, of searching for Sarah, of finding her. Then they were climbing without harnesses or ropes or anchors. She started falling, and he grasped her hand. But she refused to grasp his other hand, and he couldn't hold on. Couldn't save her. Her hand slipped from his, and she was gone.

It didn't take a psychiatrist to interpret that one.

His mind adjusted along with his eyes. Darkness still cloaked the dining room, sunrise just starting to pink the sky through windows facing east. A rustle of movement came from the next booth.

"Sarah?" he whispered.

"Yeah?"

"Did you hear something?"

"I…I don't know. What was it?"

He levered himself off the bench and onto his feet. He wasn't sure. It didn't make sense for construction crews to be here so early, did it? And on a Sunday? "A rattle, maybe. Like someone opening the lock."

Sarah climbed out of her booth as well. "Front or back?"

He tried to recreate the sound in his memory. "I'm not sure, but I'm betting back." He grabbed the backpack from where he left it after refilling the water bottles. He strained to hear more, the creak of a door, a footstep.

A clatter rose from the kitchen.

Eric gestured to Sarah with a tilt of his head. He set off for the back dining room, trying to keep his footsteps as quiet as possible on the tile. He could hear Sarah follow behind, running on her toes. He didn't want to jump to conclusions about who might be in a closed restaurant this early. It could simply be a manager. An owner. Someone working on the renovations. If the police had tracked them down, they would have stormed the place last night, wouldn't they?

Not that it mattered. If whoever was here found them, their first move would be to call the police, and it wouldn't take a brain surgeon to figure out the woman and man who were camped out in the dining room of a closed restaurant probably weren't your average tourists.

"You sure it's in here?"

Behind him, Sarah jumped at the male

voice echoing from the waiter's station outside the kitchen.

Eric grabbed her arm and ducked behind the back dining room's open door.

Two young men dressed in jeans, boots and hats swaggered between tables. The way they were dressed probably ruled out construction workers, and they didn't look nearly old enough to own or run a place like this. If Eric had to guess, he'd put them at barely out of high school. They passed the doorway and headed toward the bar.

Eric pushed up from the wall just as the tinkling sound of a giggle followed in the boys' wake.

He flattened back into the shadow. Sarah did the same. Seconds seemed to stretch longer than minutes before two girls walked past, heels clacking unsteadily on tile. They didn't spare as much as a glance in Eric and Sarah's direction.

Eric let a relieved breath stream through his lips.

The foursome crowded behind the bar where Eric had pilfered the bottle of cocktail cherries the night before. "Is there any beer?" a male voice said.

"Beer? Ain't you had enough beer? We got some good whiskey here. Look at this."

"Can you make Sex on the Beach?" one of the girls asked.

Now was their chance. Eric nodded to Sarah, and they made their way to the fire exit at the back of the dining room. Bracing himself for an alarm, Eric pushed the door open.

No sound but the predawn tweet of birds met his ears.

The two of them rushed outside. The cool morning air felt like a slap to hot cheeks. Eric stopped dead in his tracks and stared.

A gray SUV that should have been junked long ago sat outside the kitchen entrance, no doubt waiting while its driver and his friends stole some liquor so they could continue their party.

And the engine was still running.

"Sarah? I found something. You're not going to believe this."

The tension in Eric's voice zinged along Sarah's nerves and curled in her chest like a spring. They'd only had one free computer at the tiny library, so she'd let Eric take the Google honors, pulling a chair up next to him to see what he turned up. Unfortunately the morning light streaming through the front window was making the print on the screen fade into oblivion.

She shifted on her chair, perching on the edge of one hip and leaning forward. From here, she could smell Eric's shampoo and the soap they'd picked up at an area Wal-Mart. They'd used some of their money to buy new shirts, too, and cheap jackets, although they didn't have enough for new jeans. They'd showered at a campground, and Eric had even shaved. Between that and a box of hair dye that changed his hair from sandy to dark, he looked like a different man. But although she'd considered cutting her own hair, she'd settled on plaiting it into a thick braid, a move that always accentuated the tiny bit of her ancestry that was Native American.

What she failed to pick up was a pair of sunglasses. She squinted against the glare, trying to see the newspaper story on his screen. "Where?"

He pointed to a spot midway through the article. "Woman killed in a car accident eight years ago. Driver left the scene. He was caught by matching fingerprints in the stolen car to prints police had on file. The woman's name was Marion Strub."

She leaned toward him a little more, sensing a punch line coming.

"Her maiden name was Gillette." He turned and looked at her, the glow from the screen making his green eyes look electric against his new dark hair.

"The sheriff's sister?"

"That's right." He looked back to the screen. "Sister of Norris County Sheriff Daniel Gillette."

So his sister had been killed in an accident. She hadn't remembered that. Of course, eight years ago, she hadn't had a lot of reason to think about Sheriff Danny Gillette. She hadn't even voted for him. "And Larry Hodgeson? Is there some connection with the fingerprints?"

"That's how I found the story. Hodgeson matched the prints and testified in the drunk driver's trial."

She searched her mind, trying to come up with a reason that could lead to the sheriff wanting Hodgeson dead. She knew she felt a sharp need for the men who killed Randy to pay for what they'd done. Maybe Gillette felt that way, too. "And the driver got off?"

"Nope. He had a long history of driving drunk, and he was slam-dunked by the fingerprints. He got fifteen years. He's still in the state pen in Rawlins."

"Then how—" She caught the glare of the librarian at the circulation desk across the room. She hadn't spoken above a whisper, but apparently, even that was too loud. She gave the woman a sheepish smile and mouthed *I'm sorry,* then brought her finger to her lips, warning Eric. The last thing they needed was to draw attention. She'd almost blown it. She lowered her voice until she could barely hear it herself. "How does that explain anything?

"It doesn't. But at least we have a connection between them."

There had to be something more. Hodgeson worked a lot of criminal cases. Surely there had to be more fingerprints from cases in Norris County that went to the state crime lab for analysis. Something.

"Got another hit on Hodgeson. But this trial didn't take place in Norris County."

"What is it about?"

He held up a hand as he read the story.

She squinted, straining to make out the words through the glare. She wished she could stand and lean over Eric's shoulder, but that might make her more noteworthy to the librarian. She didn't dare risk it. Besides, being that close to Eric, smelling his scent, moving her face next to his...bad idea.

Eric glanced up at her. "It's a drug case. Methamphetamine. Police found a trailer home that was being used as a meth lab. A guy named Walter Burne owned the land and the double-wide, but his prints didn't end up matching the prints inside. The jury decided that added up to reasonable doubt."

"And Hodgeson analyzed the fingerprints?"

"Yeah. But there's no connection to Gillette. Not that I can see here." He grabbed for the mouse, and clicked back to the search window.

Something shifted in Sarah's memory. "Wait."

Eric paused.

"Go back to that last story."

He did as she asked.

"What was the guy's name?"

"Walter Burne. You know it?"

She did, didn't she? "Is it spelled with an *e* on the end?"

"Yeah."

"There's a guy named Burne at the Full Throttle. Spells his name with an *e*. I don't know his first name."

"You're drinking at biker bars now?"

"It's not a biker bar, really. Not anymore. But it's still a rough place. Maybe rougher than it used to be. The guy named Burne is the new owner."

Eric shook his head and stared at her as if she were speaking a language he couldn't understand. "Biker bar, rough bar, what are you doing hanging around at a place like that at all?"

"I wasn't. Randy was. It was the first place he went when he got out of jail. Keith saw him there, was worried he was up to no good. And he said he'd also seen Randy with this Burne guy back before his arrest." She hadn't taken Keith's warnings very seriously. The kid had an ax to grind with just about anyone, it seemed. She merely told him she'd talk to Randy about it. And she had meant to the next day…after he returned from Saddle Horn Ridge.

Eric tented his fingers in front of his lips. "Maybe Gillette's not the connection. Randy is."

Sarah nodded, regret stinging her eyes. She blinked back moisture in time to see the librarian abandon the circulation desk and start walking their way.

Chapter Thirteen

"She might just be going to warn us to keep it down." Sarah's whisper quavered.

She might be right, but Eric wasn't about to count on it. He noted the name of the reporter who wrote the article was the same as the last one and clicked the mouse, bringing the computer back to the blank search screen. "I'll talk to her. Get up and head for the bathroom. Take the back exit like we planned."

"Not without you."

"It's not like she can physically stop me from leaving. I'll meet you at the SUV. Go."

Sarah pushed out of her chair and walked for the hall that housed the restrooms…and the back exit door.

They'd known a trip to the library was risky. Although he didn't yet know what to make of what they'd found, he hoped the risk was worth it. Better yet, he hoped they were wrong about the librarian's motives.

He looked up at the woman and smiled.

She smiled back as she approached, laugh lines creasing tanned skin. A short-sleeved blouse showed muscular arms. Probably in her fifties, she looked less like the stereotypical librarian and more like an outdoors enthusiast.

"I apologize if we were too loud. We're on our way out."

"That's not why I came over."

"Oh?"

"You just look so familiar to me. I was wondering if I know you from somewhere."

Yes, probably from those news reports you've watched. He forced a laugh. "That always happens to me. You're the third person who's said that this week. My wife says I have a generic face."

She laughed and pushed curly hair back from her cheek. "Sorry to bother you."

Eric let out a breath as she walked away. When she reached her spot at the circulation desk, she turned back to take another look.

He had to get out of here.

He pushed to his feet and casually walked to the restroom. At least he hoped it looked casual. He felt like his nerves were jumping out of his skin. When he reached the hall, he bolted past the marked doors and went straight for the red exit sign.

Sarah sat in the passenger seat of the SUV. Eric slid behind the wheel and started the engine just as the library door opened and the librarian stuck her head out the door.

Great. He pressed the gas and drove. Not too fast. Nothing to see here.

"That was close," Sarah said as they turned on to the highway. "What did she say?"

"She thought she recognized me."

"Did she figure out why?"

"Don't know. But even if she didn't just take down our license plate, we're going to have to come up with a new ride. Driving a stolen truck is pushing our luck." Too bad. Eric liked the feeling of control having a vehicle once again gave him. Of course he knew it was an illusion. He didn't really have control of anything. But the act of researching connections, uncovering pieces of the truth, as small as they were, at least made him *feel* like he was getting somewhere. Taking charge of something. Fighting back.

Taking steps to protect Sarah and the baby.

"Maybe we can find something to drive at the Full Throttle."

He glanced at Sarah out of the corner of his eye. "Conviction or not, Burne seems to be a meth dealer. There's no telling what Randy got himself into with someone like that. You sure you want to go there?"

"I don't see how we have a lot of choice. If we can't get help from law enforcement, maybe it's time to try the other side of the equation."

He nodded in agreement, but he didn't like the desperate tone in her voice.

SARAH SQUINTED THROUGH thick smoke at the half-dozen or so men spending a Sunday afternoon drinking in the hazy dimness of the Full Throttle. Two wore cowboy hats. Most sported prison tattoos. None of them looked friendly. She'd dealt with hard-edged men her entire life, but she was glad Eric was with her all the same.

She and Eric stepped to the bar. The place smelled of stale smoke, stale beer and sanitizer, probably stale as well. A bartender zeroed in on them. Face overwhelmed by a handlebar mustache he must have started growing when they were in style in the early 1900s, he slapped a bar towel down and leaned forward on meaty palms. "What can I get ya?" He ran an assessing gaze over Sarah.

She ignored whatever demeaning message he was trying to send. "Are you Walter Burne?"

The man chuckled. "Do I look like Burne?"

"I don't know. What does Burne look like?"

"Not like me. Now what are you drinking?"

"Did you know Randy Trask?"

He gave a disgusted roll of his eyes. "You sure as hell ask a lot of questions."

"Did you know him?"

"Maybe. Who are you?"

"I'm his sister."

She could feel Eric tense up.

She knew it was dangerous, letting anyone know who she was. She wasn't sure if her name and photo were being broadcast alongside Eric's, but she wouldn't be surprised. Layton was pretty adamant that the sheriff wanted her just as much. He never would have encouraged her to run otherwise. But as nervous as she was about identifying herself, she had little choice. She doubted she'd get anywhere with this guy by playing coy games. Besides, she'd bet the patrons of the Full Throttle wanted a visit from the sheriff about as much as she did. She needed to take a chance.

"The rancher lady." A smile curved beneath all the hair, teasing, knowing, cruel. "Well, Randy ain't here. But then, you probably know that."

A man down the bar stood and moved several stools closer. "Why are you looking for Randy? He's dead."

"We're not looking for Randy," Eric said. "We're looking for people who knew him."

"Ahh." The newcomer to the conversation chuckled deep in his skinny chest, the sound infused with the rattle of someone who was a long-time smoker. He perched on the edge of the stool. His leg bounced, as if he was itching to move. "I might have known him."

Even though he was sitting, Sarah could tell he was close to Eric's height. But where Eric was fit and built with more than his share of muscle, this guy was narrow as a wire. And judging from his jumpy demeanor, she'd say a live wire at that.

The kind of nervous energy that might have come from dipping in to the drugs he produced? "Are you Burne?"

"Me? Ha! You've got to be out of your mind."

"Who are you?"

"Name's Jerry."

"Sarah." She held out her hand and they

shook. His palm was moist, and Sarah fought the urge to wipe her hand on her jeans. "Were you here when Randy came in the other day?"

"What, after he got out?"

"Yes."

"Maybe. Don't remember."

"Well, have you heard what he stopped in here about?"

"Having a drink isn't a good reason for stopping in a bar?" the bartender boomed. He leveled a look on them, a clear hint they should order if they intended to stay.

"Give us a Sprite and a tapper." Eric threw a ten on the bar.

Sarah turned back to the guy on the next bar stool. "Was there any other reason Randy came in here? Something *besides* having a drink?"

"Don't know whatcha mean." He folded arms that were little more than flesh stretched over bone across his chest. Tattoos marked his pale skin with thick black lines. Not the most delicate work Sarah had seen by a long shot. They looked as if they were done with make-shift equipment and an untalented hand.

"Looks like you've done some time yourself." Eric gestured to the tats Sarah had noticed. "What can you tell us about a guy named Bracco?"

"Bracco?" The guy glanced around the bar as if his overabundance of energy had deteriorated into paranoia. "Never heard of him."

"He was Randy's cell mate," Eric supplied.

"How would I know Randy's cellie? It's not like I was in at the same time." He drew himself up and pushed out his bony chest. "Besides, Randy was just in county. I've done real time."

"Something to be proud of, no doubt." Sarah did her best not to roll her eyes as the bartender had at her. But as ridiculous as this guy's pride over his record was, maybe she could use it to her advantage. "I think you know him. I think you're scared."

He pulled in his chin like a surprised turtle. He shifted his weight backward and the bar stool creaked under him. "Scared? Why would I be scared of Bracco? He's dead."

Eric narrowed his eyes. "You sure about that?"

"Offed himself in his cell. Happened before Christmas."

Sarah added this piece to the puzzle in her mind. If Bracco told Randy something was on Saddle Horn Ridge, he must have done it when her brother was first sentenced.

"What makes you think it was suicide?" asked Eric.

"That's what the papers said."

"And you don't find that a little strange?"

"I guess. Hardened guys usually don't off themselves like that, if that's what you're getting at."

That had been exactly what Eric was getting at. It wasn't a suicide. Sarah looked up at him. The sheriff must have killed Bracco, too. Only before he died, he told Randy there was something up on Saddle Horn Ridge. Something valuable worth finding. Was it possible?

She lowered a hip to the bar stool next to Jerry. The question was, how did Bracco know Larry Hodgeson's body was on that ridge? "What was Bracco arrested for?"

Jerry spun back and forth on the stool, as if it was beyond him to sit still. "How the hell should I know? Some damn thing."

"You said he was a hardened guy, that he'd been in before."

"So?"

The bartender set her soda and Eric's beer on the bar. He reached out for the money.

"So what was he in for?" she asked.

Jerry waved his hand in front of his face, as if clearing the air of the bad smell her question brought with it. "Don't they have records you can look up? I've talked with you people so much, my throat is getting parched." He eyed the drinks sitting on the bar.

Eric nodded to bartender and motioned to their skinny, pale friend. "Whatever he wants."

The bartender leveled a bored look on their companion. "What'll it be, Jer?"

"Your best whiskey. A double. And a beer to chase it."

Eric fished out his wallet and threw the last of their cash on the bar.

A chill moved over Sarah's skin. So that was it. They could no longer pay their way. Couldn't buy a drink or a sandwich or a clean shirt. They were forced to be criminals all the way, now.

The bartender plunked Jerry's double shot and beer on the bar, and the skinny man took a long drink of whiskey. He set the highball glass down and reached for the beer.

Eric slid the glass out of Jerry's reach. "First, Bracco."

Jerry let out a wheezy sigh. "Rumor has it, he took care of problems for a price."

"Problems?" Sarah asked. "What kind of problems?"

Eric kept his hand on Jerry's beer. "By problems, you mean he killed people for money?"

"Killed people, cleaned up messes, whatever needed to be done. Can I have my beer back?" He reached out, and Eric slid the beer into his palm.

Sarah's mind raced. So was that how this Bracco knew where to find Larry Hodgeson's body? He'd pulled the trigger? Had the sheriff hired him to do his dirty work?

"Do you know a man named Larry Hodgeson?" Eric continued.

Jerry met his question with a blank stare. He took a chug of beer.

"He worked in the state crime lab. He analyzed fingerprints," Sarah supplied.

A light seemed to come on behind those jittery eyes.

She leaned forward. "You know him?"

"Nah. Not me." Jerry laughed, his lips pulling back to expose teeth that smelled as bad as they looked. "But Burne does. Don't ya, Burne?"

Sarah followed Jerry's gaze.

At first she thought he was looking at one of the two men standing at the back of the bar wearing cowboy hats. A man who from this distance looked very much like her ranch hand, Keith Sherwood. Then a man standing next to a pool table barely ten feet away turned around slowly.

A black leather duster fell to his knees. He stepped toward them, expensive lizard boots clunking on wood plank floor.

He skimmed his gaze down her body, but instead of the leer she got from the bartender, his expression was cold, clinical, like a rancher sizing up a steer. His black shirt was opened at the collar. Tattoos circled his throat, the ink forming intricate patterns of twisted barbed wire. "So you're Sarah Trask."

It wasn't a question, and she didn't answer.

"Glad to finally meet you. Randy often bragged about that big, profitable ranch of yours. Said you have a good business sense. Make smart decisions. Something he obviously never inherited."

The bad feeling that had been niggling at the back of Sarah's neck became a full bore bite. She hadn't liked the fact that Randy knew this guy before she'd met him. Now she liked the idea even less.

Eric stepped around her stool so he was standing by her side. "You know Larry Hodgeson?"

"Never met the man."

Yeah, right. "He was a fingerprint analyst for the Wyoming crime lab," Sarah said. "He testified at your trial."

He brought his focus back to her. His eyes gleamed cold, emotionless, brutal. As if he could kill her right now, without a second thought. Like swatting a fly. "I said I never met the man. Not that I was never in the same room with him."

Sarah set her chin. "Then why did Jerry say you did?"

"Jerry?" He threw a dismissive glance the skinny man's way. "He's a meth head. Look at him. He don't know what's going on in his own mind half the time."

Jerry sat back on the stool and clasped his hands in his lap. Where most people twiddled their thumbs, he twiddled all fingers at once. "Okay, yeah, my bad. He doesn't really know him. The guy just—"

"Shut…up."

"The guy just…" Sarah repeated, leaning toward the jittery beanpole of a man. "What did Hodgeson *just* do?"

"Listen, Sarah Trask." Burne's voice held an edge like a knife. "I don't want to talk about Larry Hodgeson."

"Hodgeson's dead. Murdered," Eric said.

Burne kept his eyes riveted on her. "So? I sure didn't do it. The guy saved my ass."

He had a point. Hadn't the online article said

that Hodgeson's testimony had caused the jury to acquit Burne? It didn't make sense for him to be involved in the fingerprint analyst's death. So where did that leave them? She couldn't believe Burne and Hodgeson and Sheriff Gillette and Randy were all tied together by coincidence. It had to add up somehow.

"Like I said, I don't want to talk about the CSI guy. I'd much rather have a chat about your brother."

Sarah's pulse picked up its pace. "What about him?"

"He owed me. And with him dead, looks like you're the one who's going to have to pay."

ERIC STRAIGHTENED HIS shoulders and stepped in front of Sarah, fully blocking her from Burne. When he'd heard Randy was involved with a guy like this, he'd been furious. And now Burne thought he could pull Sarah further into this mess? Guess again. "Randy's debts died with him."

The scumbag finally looked at him. "Not from where I'm standing." The man's hand hovered at his waist. His long leather duster reached to his knees, covering the holster Eric bet was underneath.

He couldn't win this argument, especially

not once guns were drawn. And although the prospect of walking away sent a pain shooting through his head like an ice pick to the eye, he had to remember that Sarah was the important one in all of this.

He had to get her out of here.

"Sarah doesn't know anything about what her brother was into. She can't help you."

"Well, someone is going to give me back my money. If it isn't her, who's it going to be? You?"

Sarah's fingers closed around his bicep. "How much did he owe?"

Burne leaned his face inches from Eric's and grinned. "See? No need for bluster, friend. The lady believes in paying her debts."

It was all Eric could do not to push his fingertips into the guy's eyes. He didn't know what Sarah had in mind, but if she thought this debt was a small thing she could take care of like a bar tab, he had a feeling she was going to be unpleasantly surprised.

"How much?" Sarah repeated.

"Twenty thousand."

Sarah gasped. "Twenty… Why?"

"He screwed up. Lost the money I fronted him for a sporting goods shop he wanted to open."

"Sporting goods shop, my ass," Eric growled

under his breath. He hadn't heard anything about a sporting goods shop. More likely the money was meant for expanding Burne's current business, making drugs. And knowing Randy, he'd probably blown the money. Bet it in Vegas or on football games, sure that he was going to win big, have enough to set up Burne's new meth lab and pocket the profits himself.

Sarah's eyes glistened. She looked like she was about to cry. "Randy told you he could get that much money?"

"The day he got out."

It all added up. Randy on the cliff…explaining he didn't think Bracco's warnings of danger were real…swearing the only reason he'd risked it was he owed a guy a lot of money. And apparently that guy was Burne. "How did he say he was going to get it?"

"Told me he heard about an opportunity while in county. Told me he just had to take a little hike and he'd have the money, just like that."

A little hike led by his sucker of a friend. "So that's why Randy stopped by the night he got out of jail?"

"He knew I'd be looking for him, so he came looking for me first. I like a man who shows initiative. I like a man who pays better." He motioned to Jerry and the skinny man slipped off his bar stool and stepped toward the door. Sliding into the vacated spot, Burne leaned toward Sarah and rested a hand on the bar, blocking the path in front of her. "But since sister Sarah is going to take care of that now, I guess I have no cause to curse his damned memory. So where's the money?"

"I don't have it."

"Wrong answer."

Eric's heart slammed against his ribs as if fighting to get free. Burne was a violent man, an unpredictable man. Eric could tell by the way he moved, the cold deadness in his eyes. He had to come up with a way to get Sarah away from him. "She can get it."

"Good. I'll go with you." He glanced in Eric's direction, then returned his focus to Sarah. "Just the two of us."

"There's no way in hell that's happening." Eric balled his hands into fists. He wouldn't let the meth dealer take her. There wasn't a chance.

The man gave him a smug glance. His hand moved under his duster. "Really?"

Sarah shook her head. "You can't come with me. Not unless you want to catch the sheriff's attention. He's watching my ranch. I don't even know if I can get into my house without being seen."

"Ah, yes. The two of you are wanted for your brother's murder, aren't you? All the more reason for you to pay up now. I've already waited for my money long enough. I'm not planning to wait twenty to life. So I suggest you find a way. Now." He pushed the duster back with one hand, flashing a semiautomatic handgun strapped to his hip, buckle of the holster popped open, ready to draw. Just as quickly, the duster settled back over the gun.

The move was fast, fluid, even casual, as if showing the gun was an absentminded accident. Eric knew it was anything but. It was a threat, pure and simple. If Sarah didn't get the money, she was dead.

Footsteps scuffled outside the room. Jerry stood in the doorway looking like he was about to climb out of his skin. "They're here."

Burne raised black brows. "Who?"

"Sheriff's deputies. Flashing lights. They're pulling into the parking lot right now."

Chapter Fourteen

In a flash of movement, Burne grabbed Sarah by the braid and pulled her head back, cradling her against his chest like a lover.

Eric surged forward. He wasn't going to let Burne hurt her. Damn it, he wasn't going to let the scumbag *touch* her.

An arm came from behind him, a knife blade flashing inches from his face. "I wouldn't do that." The bartender's beer-tainted breath fanned his face.

Eric's mind stuttered. He hadn't seen the guy move out from behind the bar. He'd been caught flat-footed, unprepared.

Burne pressed his cheek against Sarah's. "Have my money by noon tomorrow, all twenty grand, or the sheriff will be the least of your problems. Understand?"

She glared at him.

"Understand?"

"Yes."

"You'll get a call telling you where to meet. You'd better answer." He shoved something into her hand, released her hair and pushed her away.

Sarah stumbled against a bar stool, clutching a cell phone in her fist. She scrambled to regain her balance. Eric tried to move toward her, but the bartender's hand clamped down hard on his shoulder. The blade pressed cold just below his ear.

"Get out of here," Burne said. "Through the back. The last thing I need is for you to be arrested before I get paid. Go."

The knife pulled back. The arm released Eric. He focused on Burne, that smug face, those brutal eyes. When he'd grabbed Sarah he'd awakened something primal in Eric. The urge to rip a man's tattooed throat with his bare hands. But as much as he wanted to stuff those threats back from where they'd come, he needed to get Sarah out of there more. He needed to protect her from Burne, all right, but he couldn't forget the sheriff.

He grabbed Sarah's hand. They dodged the pool table and raced for the back door. The men in cowboy hats he'd noticed standing in the back of the bar were gone. Cleared out. Before Jerry had yelled his warning or after, Eric didn't know.

They reached the door and Eric pulled it open. As soon as they pushed out into the clear basin wind, Eric could hear the bark of male voices coming from the front of the building. A white SUV sat in the gravel drive, blocking all vehicles from leaving. Sheriff's deputies stood among the vehicles in the lot.

So much for dumping their stolen SUV. And inside the SUV was the backpack with the belt buckle inside. Damn.

"We have to go on foot." Before the words were out of his mouth, they were racing across the gravel and into land dotted with sagebrush and dry tufts of grass. A quarry gaped behind the bar like a wound, the land gashed and marred by heavy machinery. Reaching the pounded dirt road, they followed it, running for all they were worth.

With every stride, Eric prayed Burne was serious about wanting his money, serious enough to stall the sheriff until they got away. Relying on the man who'd just threatened Sarah to save them tasted as acidic as bile in the back of Eric's throat. But at this point, he'd take any help they could get.

Sarah pointed to a flat-topped hill on the other side of the gaping quarry pit. "Everything beyond that bench is BLM land. It backs up to the ranch." She panted each word, the rhythm of her strides slowing.

The ranch. Reaching the far side of the mine, Eric pulled Sarah behind a pile of gravel. There, sheltered from the view of the men back at the tavern, he slowed to a walk, giving Sarah a chance to catch her breath. They needed a plan. "How far is the ranch?"

"Not far. Probably less than two miles."

"You have other vehicles there, right? Another ATV?"

She nodded. Leaning forward, she braced her hands on her knees. "You think they won't be watching it?"

"Not if they're tied up at the bar." He knew it was risky, but he'd managed to sneak into the ranch undetected once before. And Sarah knew the land better than anyone. "Where are your hands? Layton?"

"Should be out on the BLM, checking the cattle. They would have taken the horses, though, not the ATV. Layton's preference."

"Good."

"Say we manage to get the ATV and get out without being seen, where do we go from there?"

"Not sure. We'll figure it out. But in the

meantime, I know a place. A friend's cabin. No one will be there until about a week before the parks open. We can stay there." It had been the place he'd thought about at the beginning. A place where they could hole up. See no one. A place where he could keep Sarah safe until they sorted out this mess and decided what to do next.

The hike to the ranch didn't take long by Wyoming standards. They ran most of the way, a steady jog. The sun was just settling low in the sky when they crossed the fence line and started through the east pasture. By the time the house and outbuildings came into view, twilight still glowed over the mountains to the west.

"God, it seems so long ago…I used to feel so safe here. I wonder if I ever will again."

The ache in Sarah's voice settled into Eric's bones. She had told him about her feelings for the ranch before. Said it was her rock. The only thing she could rely on between her parents' turmoil and the problems Randy stirred up everywhere he went.

Now she'd lost the ranch, too.

He wanted nothing more than to get it back for her. Maybe it was possible. He had to believe it was. But possible or not, clearing their names was still a long way off and would require more than a few miracles. The best he could do right now was to get his hands on that ATV and use it to get her someplace safe for the night. "Come on."

The place felt as vacant as it had when he'd rescued her from the sheriff. Not a body around. No movement but the horses in the corral. And this time—thankfully—no sign of the sheriff's SUV.

With any luck, he'd be tied up with Burne and his criminal drinking buddies for a good long while.

Sarah led the way to a freestanding garage on the other side of the house. She twisted the manual garage door's handle and Eric helped her slide the door up on its overhead tracks.

They stared at the back bumper of a blue pickup.

Eric didn't recognize the truck. He glanced at Sarah. "Yours?"

"No. I think—"

"You move, you're dead."

Eric turned. The barrel of a rifle was leveled straight at Sarah's forehead.

"GLENN." SARAH'S FIRST URGE was to hug her ranch hand. Her second was that although he wasn't the sheriff, that didn't mean they were home free. "What are you doing here?"

"God, Sarah. I almost shot you." He tilted his hat back from his forehead and lowered his gun from his shoulder, but he didn't avert the barrel, as if he wasn't quite sure what he should do.

"Glenn, listen. This whole thing you've heard about Randy's death. It's not true."

"I know you didn't have nothing to do with killing Randy."

"You know?" She'd expected him to say a lot of things, mostly reciting platitudes about justice and doing the right thing. She'd never expected this.

Glenn glanced at Eric. "Layton thinks it was all him."

"Eric didn't do it, either, Glenn."

He pressed his lips together, making his cheeks bulge on either side of his mouth. Everything about Glenn was square, from his boxy legs to his shoulders to the shape of his head. And nothing was more square than his attitude toward the law.

Sarah had to find a way to convince him. "Layton is wrong. It was the sheriff and two of his men who killed Randy. They were trying to cover up another murder, and Randy got too close."

Glenn pointed the barrel at the ground and rubbed his sweaty forehead. "I wondered what the hell was going on."

"What?" Eric stepped forward. "Do you know something about the sheriff?"

Glenn looked from Eric back to Sarah. His square shoulders slumped a little, as if it was taking a lot out of him to face what he was about to tell them. "I heard Sheriff Gillette talking to Keith. Said something about getting justice."

"Getting justice? For what?"

"I don't know. Every damn thing."

Sarah didn't know what to think. Here she thought Glenn was the law-and-order guy. The man who loved cop shows and novels. The man who wanted to be a cop and would do anything to help someone like the sheriff, if he believed his cause was just. She always thought Keith was built more along the lines of a vigilante. The perfect recruit for a homegrown militia group, maybe, but a man who chafed at government and had no patience for law. "How did Keith react?"

"He has the kid all fired up. It's all Keith can talk about. People getting what they deserve and what all."

She pictured the cowboy hat at the back of

the smokey bar. The shaggy blond hair and rangy face underneath. She glanced at Eric. "I thought I saw him at the Full Throttle just now."

"The cowboy hat at the back."

She nodded.

"Don't surprise me. He left the ranch around lunchtime and didn't come back. He ain't been anywhere he's supposed to lately."

Sarah straightened. Things were starting to add up, and she didn't like where they were going. "There were other times he left work? When?"

Glenn adjusted his hat with one hand. "Man, I don't know."

She did. "The day Randy was killed?"

He narrowed his eyes and stared at the garage wall, as if counting back in his mind. "Was that the day we took the herd out to the BLM?"

Sarah nodded. She had a feeling she might know what was coming. A bad feeling. She braced herself.

"Yeah, he disappeared that day."

"When?"

"After we loaded up. Didn't even say where he was going. Layton went out to look for him, but never found him. I had to unload the cattle alone."

She glanced at Eric, trying to read if he was thinking the same thing. Then she brought her focus back to Glenn. "Has Keith said anything else to you?"

"Like what?"

"I don't know, anything about Randy or a place called Saddle Horn Ridge?"

"He talked about Randy. How he saw him at the Full Throttle talking to some drug dealer."

Sarah nodded. "He told me that, too."

"How about a man named Larry Hodgeson?" Eric asked. "Has Keith mentioned him?"

Glenn started to shake his head, then paused.

"Think of something?" Sarah fought the urge to lean toward him and grab his shoulders, shake him into remembering whatever it was that made him pause.

"Yeah. Hodgeson. He was in the news a while back, wasn't he?"

"He has been. Did Keith mention him?"

"Yeah. Last summer he was all mad. Said this Hodgeson took a payoff to let some drug dealer go, and now he was going to make things even worse. Keith said people like this Hodgeson were what was wrong with law enforcement. Is Hodgeson a cop or something?" Glenn's eyebrows pinched together, as if he wasn't sure he wanted the answer.

"No."

Glenn let out a shaky breath.

Sarah's mind whirled with Glenn's words. *Make things even worse?* Hodgeson no longer worked for the crime lab. He hadn't for years. How could Hodgeson make things worse?

"We'd better get out of here, Sarah." Eric's voice cut through her thoughts. "Where's the ATV?"

She pointed to the other side of the garage.

"Tell you what," Glenn said. "Why don't you take my truck?"

She scanned his face. He seemed sincere. Like he wanted to help. But if she couldn't trust one of her hands, could she really afford to trust the other?

"Things are strange around here," Glenn said. "Real strange. I don't know what to think, but I don't think you'd kill your brother. And I don't want to see you pay for something you'd never do."

She nodded. She hadn't thought anything bad about Glenn Freemont in the time he'd worked for her. Not until this mess. But he really was a good guy. And he really did seem to care about her. It felt good to know she'd been right about someone. That everyone she knew wasn't harboring some secret that would come back to hurt her. "Thanks, Glenn." She gave him a hug, and he slipped the truck's keys into her hand.

Eric wheeled the ATV to the mouth of the garage. "Let's take this, too. It'll give us some flexibility."

After Glenn helped Eric heave the vehicle into the pickup bed, she passed the keys to Eric and climbed into the passenger seat. A second later, they were speeding out of the gravel driveway and down the road. For a moment, she just stared out the window at the landscape rolling by, trying to absorb how little she knew about some people in her life. Randy. Now Keith. "Do you think Keith is in on this thing with the sheriff, whatever it is?"

"Could be. Or Glenn is."

"Glenn?" She shook her head. She must not have heard him right. "Why Glenn?"

"Think about it. The only thing we know about Keith Sherwood is what Glenn told us."

"And that he was at the Full Throttle."

"Which means nothing. From the sound of it, he hangs out there all the time."

"True."

"And being out at the Full Throttle ties Keith to Burne more than the sheriff. Either that or he just has a simple drinking problem."

"Good point. But none of that suggests Glenn has anything to hide. He helped us. Gave us his truck."

Eric nodded. "His truck, which is equipped with a GPS."

Sarah gasped and held her hands against her chest. Again she'd been so trusting. So blind. That Glenn had been offering his truck for a reason, to trap them, had never occurred to her. "You think the sheriff is using it to track us?"

"Not anymore. I turned the damn thing off."

Chapter Fifteen

Eric didn't want to take a chance.

They took Glenn's truck as far as the campground outside Norris. There, they left it among a dozen vehicles belonging to early summer tourists and hiked the rest of the way to his guide friend's cabin on foot.

The cabin wasn't exactly rustic, more like a tiny house on the outside of town than a real cabin. But the neighbors were few and far between, no one in the area nosed into others' business, and most important of all, he knew where to find the key.

Throughout the entire trek, all Eric could think about was their close call at the Full Throttle. How little control of the situation he'd had. How he'd almost lost Sarah for good. Add that to what had happened with Glenn Freemont, and he was reeling.

He needed to put an end to this. And he would do whatever it took.

He found the cabin's key hidden in its usual place under a flap of loose siding, opened the door and ushered Sarah inside.

The cabin was tiny, only one real room. One end of it formed a small kitchen, the other a living area with a full sized bed in one corner and a television in the other. Definitely a bachelor pad. A bathroom the size of a closet was tucked against the wall.

The place smelled dusty, the air dead. At least out here the weather was so dry they didn't have to worry about mustiness and mildew. But it wasn't exactly homey. "Dev probably hasn't been here for a while. We'll have to keep our eyes out for scorpions and black widows."

She nodded, unfazed. "It's nice."

"I don't know about that, but it's safe. At least for a while."

She gave him a sad smile. "These days 'safe' is the same as nice to me."

He knew the feeling.

Sarah strolled deeper into the cabin. He followed her in time to see her lower herself to the bed and let out an exhausted sigh. For a second, he had the urge to sit beside her, to take her in his arms, to lay her down and show her how much he wanted to take care of her. How much he had changed.

"There's only one bed," she said.

Warmth fanned out over his skin. He'd like to think that by the tone in her voice, she was thinking the same thing. But he'd probably be fooling himself. Last night in the restaurant, she'd told him she couldn't take a chance on him. He doubted anything had changed. At least not with her.

He was a different story.

With every minute Eric was with her, he grew more sure she was what he wanted. Her and the baby. Maybe the turmoil he felt just wasn't that big of a deal to him in light of the crazy turn their lives had taken, a simple matter of perspective. Maybe moments where he could glimpse what it would be like to lose her had made him want to hold her that much more. Maybe the thought of the baby—of a family—was responsible for his change of heart, but he didn't think so.

The maelstrom of emotion that came with caring about her, of maybe even falling in love with her, made him feel as if he was climbing without the safety of a belay, but it also made him feel more alive than ever before. And like climbing, dangerous or not, he wanted more.

God help him, he wanted everything.

"What about this money Burne says I need to pay?" Sarah's voice didn't sound inviting this time. It sounded shaken. Scared. She held the cell phone Burne had given her, turning it over and over in her fingers. "How am I ever going to come up with it with the sheriff watching? I can't exactly walk into a bank."

Eric shoved his thoughts to the back of his mind. It wasn't the time for fantasy. Even if by some miracle Sarah decided to give him another chance, he couldn't take it until she was safe. Until this was over.

His stomach clenched at the thought of the dead-eyed meth dealer, the way he'd threatened Sarah. The way he'd touched her, pulling her head back by her braid. The way Eric had had to just stand there and watch with a knife to his throat. But as much as he'd like to take care of that guy, they couldn't get distracted. Having all law enforcement in the state of Wyoming after them made a single drug dealer seem insignificant. They had to solve the more pressing problems first. "Burne is the least of our troubles."

"Do you think Randy was selling drugs? Or making them? Do you think that's why he was in debt?" Her voice dipped to just above a whisper, as if she didn't want anyone to hear, even though there was no one around but them.

Maybe she just didn't want to hear her own questions and the answers that likely went with them. He couldn't blame her one bit.

Eric lowered himself to the mattress next to her. Just a few seconds ago, he was thinking about rolling around on the bed together. He still wanted that, but now he needed more. To comfort her. Reassure her. Make everything all right, something he knew he could never fully do.

Randy had brought Sarah a lot of worry and pain. To think he'd stooped to depths so vile in his quest for easy money was hard to reconcile with the brother she loved. Something like that was hard enough for Eric to swallow about the man he'd thought of as his friend. "Was he selling drugs? I don't know. Maybe we'll never know for sure."

"Maybe…or maybe that's what this whole thing is about. Burne, Randy, Larry Hodgeson, the sheriff—maybe they're all involved in drugs or profiting from drug money."

He considered this. "It's possible. Only it

didn't seem like Burne was very eager to see the sheriff this afternoon."

Sarah looked down at the phone clasped in her hands. "Burne wants his money before the sheriff gets ahold of us. That could change things."

"Money can change a lot of things." He thought of Hodgeson, of the fingerprint evidence in the case against Burne. "Maybe Hodgeson was bought. Maybe the sheriff was, too. But that doesn't tell us why Gillette would want Hodgeson dead or want to cover up the murder."

"And it doesn't explain Burne, either. Even if someone found out he paid Hodgeson off, he can't be tried on the drug charge again, can he?"

"I suppose he could face bribery charges, if they can prove it."

"Would he kill for that? I don't know. But if not, neither the sheriff nor Burne had a reason to kill Hodgeson." She sounded as bereft as when he sat down.

Some comfort he was. Of course, he doubted anything but answers would provide comfort for Sarah. "They didn't have a reason that we have found. Not yet, anyway."

She raised her eyes to his. "So how do we find it?"

He thought of the library, the detail in the

articles he'd read about Hodgeson. He glanced at the phone in her hand. "We call the reporter who wrote about those cases. Dennis Prohaska."

"You think that's the writer Joy was talking about? The one she said was giving her husband a big head?"

"I don't know. But if he isn't, he might know who is." He pushed himself up from the bed and crossed the room. He opened one cabinet near the phone, then another. Sure enough, there was a big fat telephone book. He called the number for the *Wyoming Tribune-Eagle*. Although they wouldn't give him the reporter's phone number, they promised to pass along the message.

"It's urgent," Eric said. "It has to do with the manhunt for that murderer. If he'd like an exclusive interview, I can arrange it. Tell him to call back at this number right away."

Prohaska called back within the hour. They had eaten some canned chili and turned on the television while they waited, and Eric stepped into the kitchen so he could focus on the call. Sarah stayed in the living area, watching him. "Thank you for calling," Eric said. "I have a few questions."

"I usually ask the questions." His voice was

brusque over the phone, in a hurry. "I thought you had information about the manhunt for Eric Lander."

"Bear with me, will you?" He took a deep breath and held Sarah's gaze. "What can you tell me about Larry Hodgeson? He's a finger-print analyst with the state crime lab."

Silence.

At first Eric thought the reporter had hung up on him. Then the soft whoosh of an expelled breath shuddered over the line. "Why are you asking about Hodgeson?" His voice was mea-sured, interested, whatever he'd been in a hurry about forgotten.

"You know the man?"

"Of course I know him. I've covered Wyoming criminal trials for years."

"When is the last time you heard from him?"

"He's retired. I haven't heard anything from him in almost a year."

Almost a year. "So you had contact with him after his retirement?" He met Sarah's big brown eyes.

"I really need to know who this is. What does this have to do with the manhunt?"

Now it was Eric's turn to be silent. Apparently his questions about Hodgeson had struck some kind of chord with the reporter. "Why are you so protective of Hodgeson?"

"Not protective. Curious. Hodgeson was a special project of mine."

A special project? Eric's mind raced, trying to figure out what that could mean.

"Who is this? Can I meet you, face-to-face?"

"Not possible." Maybe Eric could get the reporter to give him what he needed if he came at it from another angle. "What about Walter Burne? What can you tell me about him?"

"He was arrested for producing and selling methamphetamine a good five, six years ago. He was acquitted."

"And Larry Hodgeson worked on that case," Eric said.

"Pick a place. I'll meet you there."

"Why are you so eager to meet?"

The reporter paused. "Okay. I'll level with you. I'm writing a book."

A book. Of course. Being the subject of a book might give anyone a big head. "About Larry Hodgeson?"

"About the Wyoming criminal justice system. But yes, partially about Larry Hodgeson. At least it used to be, before I lost contact with him. So your questions piqued my interest."

The story seemed legitimate. Still, meeting in person was risky.

"This is Eric Lander, isn't it?"

Eric bit the inside of his bottom lip. He hadn't wanted Prohaska to know who he was, but when it came right down to it, his identity probably didn't change anything.

"I won't call the law."

"How do I know that?"

"I want the story, not an arrest. You have my word."

"You're going to have to do better than that." If there was anything Eric had learned while going through this mess, it was that taking people at their word was a fool's move.

"What if I tell you that Hodgeson's disappearance wasn't random? That something happened to him, and I might know what?"

Eric pushed up from the counter and paced across the kitchen half of the room.

"Meet me. Choose a place. I'll drive through the night if I need to. The worst that could happen is it'll be a waste of your time."

No, that wasn't the worst. Eric stopped and focused on Sarah. He thought she would be hanging on his every word, trying to use them like clues to figure out the other side of the conversation. But she stood with her back to him, her attention fully absorbed by the television, both arms cradling her abdomen as if trying to protect their baby.

She must be watching news of the manhunt. Or maybe something went down at the Full Throttle.

Their close call in the tavern still trilled along his nerves. He could have lost her. Either to a drug dealer or the sheriff. He had to get some answers. Whatever the risk, it couldn't be greater than what they already faced. He had to end this craziness now. "Be in Thermopolis by noon. I'll call you and tell you where we'll meet. Give me the number for your cell."

He did. As soon as he uttered the last digit, Eric hung up.

SARAH HEARD ERIC HANG up the phone, but she didn't take her eyes from the television. Her body alternated between a hot and cold sweat. It was all she could do to take in the images on the screen. She cupped her arm over her abdomen and willed herself to stay standing.

"Sarah?" Eric strode into the room. He glanced from her to the television.

The news coverage was live, a breaking story. The headline on the bottom of screen read Murderous Fugitives Strike Again. The camera panned over wood corral fencing, a modest house, a barn she had redesigned and remodeled herself. A still image flashed on the screen. Eric's face. Hers. And then another. The face of a man she'd just seen, just talked to, just given a hug.

The smiling face of Glenn Freemont.

She didn't know anything anymore. She'd gone from being suspicious of Glenn to grateful to him and back to suspicious. And now…

She'd watched the images once already. One after another, ending with Glenn. She'd heard the newscaster's words. The story of how Glenn's body was found at her ranch, shot with his own rifle.

Now a new clip flickered on the screen. The sheriff stood in her driveway. Behind him, county vehicles crowded around the barn. Yellow crime scene tape barred the doorway, flapping in the wind. He adjusted his silver belly Stetson lower on his bald forehead. "We have a strong lead. Just as in the Randy Trask murder, we believe the perpetrators are Eric Lander and his accomplice, Sarah Trask."

Sarah's shock turned to numbness. She didn't know what to think. She didn't know what to feel. It was as if her entire life and everything she knew had been picked up by a tornado and flung into a million pieces.

"Sarah." Eric's voice was tender, solid.

She could feel his hand hovering near her arm, wanting to touch her but holding back. "It was only a few days ago that I was so excited Randy was home." Her voice sounded raspy, like it belonged to someone else, someone barely hanging on. "I thought he had a chance to turn his life around. I thought I could see the future stretching ahead."

"I know. I know."

"And now Glenn." A sob shuddered from her chest and clogged in her throat. Glenn was dead. He'd tried to help them, and now he was dead.

"It's not our fault. You know that, right?"

She knew it. She did. The sheriff or one of his men had pulled the trigger, not her, not Eric. But that didn't mean they hadn't played a role. "If he hadn't given us his truck, he'd still be alive. He'd be going home to his wife."

Tears swamped her eyes, reducing the TV screen to glowing smeary color. She could feel the moisture on her cheeks, but she didn't wipe her eyes. She needed to feel this, not deny it, not duck from it. That was the only way the horror could ever be washed away.

Eric stepped up behind her. He wrapped his arms around hers, around her belly. His chest warmed her back. "I'm so sorry, Sarah. For Randy. For Glenn. For everything that's happened."

"It's not your fault, either."

"I know. But I'm sorry everything has happened the way it has all the same."

His words flowed over her like soothing balm on a burn. She knew she shouldn't lean in to him, but her body wouldn't listen. His chest felt so solid. Like something she could depend on. His arms strong around her.

She knew she was rationalizing, brushing all her concerns about their relationship aside because she needed him right now. But she couldn't help it. She wanted to be sure of something. She wanted to be certain to her bones. And while she might not be sure of Eric's feelings, she did know hers. She loved him. Pure and simple. She had for a long time. She'd just tried not to admit it.

But right now she needed to feel it, whether he returned those feelings or not. She needed to lose herself.

She turned in his arms. Tilting her head back, she looked up at him. She couldn't ask, couldn't speak. She just had to trust he would know what she wanted. What she needed.

He moved a hand up her side to her face. With tender fingers, he skimmed over her forehead, along her cheekbone, brushing away a strand of hair that had escaped her braid. His touch moved lower, cupping her jaw. He tilted her head back and brought his mouth to hers.

She'd craved the touch of his lips for months, yearned for his taste. She opened to him. Wanting to lose herself in him. Urging him deeper.

His arm drew tight around the small of her back, and she pressed against his length. She threaded one leg around his. She knew how his bare skin would feel against hers. She knew the sounds he'd make nuzzling her breasts, the stubble on his chin rasping tender skin. She'd run those feelings over in her thoughts for months. In her dreams. And she never thought she'd get to experience them again.

"Sarah." His voice was little more than a whisper, but it rumbled through her chest. "I want you to know—"

"Shh." She pressed her lips hard against his. She didn't have a clue what he wanted to say, but she didn't want to hear it. She didn't want to know anything more than what she felt right this minute. What she knew deep in her own heart. "I want you. That's all. I just want you. Is that okay?" She brought her lips to his again.

He nodded without breaking the kiss. Trailing his hand down her neck, he encircled her with both arms, pulling her tight, no space between them.

Yes. This was what she needed. To be held. To be loved. To love him back. Even if it was only for tonight.

Heat raced over her and swept her along. He peppered kisses over her face, her neck, her collarbone. She explored his mouth, remembering. She breathed him in, the scent of his skin making her sigh deep inside.

Skimming her hands up his sides, she pulled up the hem of his shirt and slipped her palms against ridged muscle and warm skin. She'd always loved the feel of his body, and she wanted more. She wanted all of him. She slipped her fingertips under the waistband of his jeans.

He pulled back from her. Cool air surrounded her and for a second she thought he was going to push her away. She opened her eyes in time to see him pull his shirt over his head, not taking time to mess with the buttons, and toss it on the bed.

Shadows cupped around smooth muscle. He

unzipped his jeans and shucked them down his legs. Wearing nothing but a pair of briefs, he reached for her. But instead of pulling her back into his arms, he lifted her T-shirt and skimmed it over her head.

She shivered, yet she was anything but cold. Arching her back, she reached behind and unhooked her bra. Her breasts had become heavier just in the four months since she'd gotten pregnant, the nipples larger. She let the bra slide down her arms.

Eric's hands replaced the cups. He took her lips again, kissing and massaging. Slowly, he moved her to the bed. Gently, he lowered her to the mattress. She lay on her back, and he leaned over her.

His kisses grew more demanding, and Sarah answered with demands of her own. All she could sense was how much she wanted him. All she could think about was the taste of his body, the scent of him that had always driven her wild, made her forget everything and just feel.

Feel how much she wanted him. Feel how deeply she loved him. That was all that mattered. Wipe everything else away.

He laced his fingers in hers and brought her hands above her head. He moved his kisses lower, down her throat, over her collarbone. His tongue circled a sensitive nipple.

The sensation took her breath away. He flicked and kissed and sucked, then moved to the other, lavishing, taking his time.

She thought she'd go mad with want.

By the time he released her hands and littered kisses to her jeans, she wanted nothing more than to be naked. To see him naked. To feel him inside her.

He unbuckled her jeans with deft fingers. Lifting her hips off the bed, he stripped off both jeans and panties and brought his lips to her belly.

As he kissed the slight bulge of baby, tears swamped her eyes. She blinked them back, wanting to see him, to smile at him, but it was no good. She cried as he moved his lips lower, shudders of pleasure already seizing her. And when he worked his way back up her body and kissed away her tears, she thought her heart would burst.

Chapter Sixteen

Gooseberry Badlands were carved into the floor of the Big Horn Basin. Years of erosion had eaten away soft rock, leaving red, yellow and tan layered spires and canyons twenty-five feet deep. Many of the rock towers were topped by wider caps of harder rock called hoodoos, looking to Sarah a little like the formation on top of Saddle Horn Ridge. From one of the high spots among the hoodoos, the sole highway could be seen for miles stretching in either direction. A parking lot rested at the top of a circular foot trail weaving through the badlands.

Sarah and Eric had slept later than they'd planned. Tearing herself from Eric's warm arms had been one of the hardest things she'd ever done, and even now she wished she could curl up, skin to skin, and just pretend the rest of the world didn't exist.

"What are you thinking about?"

She hadn't even been aware that Eric was watching her. Suddenly she felt insecure. Exposed. Even her cheeks heated, and she hadn't blushed in years. "Last night. This morning. How I wished we were still in bed."

He moved up behind her, circling his arms around her and pulling her against his chest as he had last night before things had heated up. "I love how you think. In fact, I love everything about you, Sarah."

His words were so close to the ones she longed to hear, longed to believe, that at first she thought she must be imagining it. Dreaming it.

She reached her arms above her head and rested her hands on his shoulders. The wind whipped off the basin, buffeting against them and whistling through rock formations.

He pulled her tight. "Just think of it all being over and us living back at your ranch—you, me and the baby. Our little family."

That image brought a smile to her face. She could almost see it. Almost feel it was true. "You're looking forward to being a dad?"

"The more this seems real, the more excited I get."

Something wobbled deep in Sarah's chest. She'd always thought Eric would make a great dad. But somehow she'd never envisioned him being excited about their baby, eager for it to be born.

Had her dad been like that when her mom was pregnant with Randy?

She didn't know where the question had come from, but once it popped into her mind, she couldn't shake it. She also couldn't give it an answer.

The wobble turned to a gnawing void, something hungry, something that couldn't quite be filled. She fitted her bottom tight to Eric's groin, yearning to feel him, but layers of denim kept them separate. She wanted to strip off her clothes, for him to plunge into her, fill her like he had last night, so she could feel the same way, close and intimate and loved.

So she could finally be sure.

She shook her head and dropped her hands to her sides. Oh, sure, they could get it on right here with Prohaska on his way and maybe the entire sheriff's department behind him. What was wrong with her? This need of hers was out of place, stupid, insecure. But try as she might, she couldn't let it go.

"What's wrong, Sarah?"

"Nothing...I don't know."

He pulled her back against his chest. "It's all going to work out."

She soaked in his warmth, tried to draw it into herself, make it hers, keep it from ever going away. "I can't do this."

He turned her in his arms, eyes searching her face. "This?"

"You and me."

"Listen, soon we'll find the truth. This will all be over. And the two of us, we can take our time, let things settle in and grow naturally."

Was that the problem? Things happening too fast? God knew their romance had bloomed quickly last summer and fall. And in the past few days since they'd been reunited and were suddenly running for their lives, she'd totally lost perspective. Could she get it back after this was over? Could she then look into his eyes and *know* that he loved her?

Could she then be *sure?*

"I..." Craning her neck, she turned and looked up at him. She drank in the swirl of color in his irises, green flecked with brown. He was excited about the baby. Felt it was his duty to be a good dad. But did he really love her enough? Did it even matter as long as she couldn't make herself believe? "I'm afraid."

"It's going to be okay. We can see the highway from here, both directions." He pointed at the gray ribbon, still void of cars. "No one can sneak up on us. If Prohaska brings the sheriff along, we'll know about it in plenty of time to get away on the ATV."

She hadn't been talking about their meeting with the reporter, but she didn't know how to tell him what she really meant. That as wonderful as making love with him was and as many times as he told her he loved her, she was afraid she'd never really know if he'd come back for her or the baby.

There was really no way *to* know.

ERIC ANGLED HIS HAND to his forehead to block the midday sun's glare. He wasn't sure what had happened just now. One moment he thought he and Sarah were closer than they'd ever been. The next, she seemed gone. She was standing here physically, her butt nestled against him and driving him wild, but something was different. She'd grown distant. Closed off. The very pressure in the air had changed.

He wasn't sure how to take it.

His whole life he'd relied on logic, reason, preparation and hard work to see him through. And it had worked. It had protected him from the chaos. It didn't make for an exciting life—instead his was measured and safe. But that was fine by him. He could get his excitement scaling a challenging rock face or viewing a waterfall human eyes might never have seen before. It suited him fine.

The past days, though, everything had changed. Each time he thought he had things under control, each time he thought he was relying on logic, he'd been wrong. But feelings…they were all he could be sure of anymore. Namely his feelings for Sarah. When he'd told her he loved everything about her, he wasn't lying.

Wind whistled through the rock formations above them, every few seconds gusting nearly as loud as a freight train. She pointed to a little blue coupe creeping along the highway. "He's here."

Eric studied the approaching vehicle. With the windshield reflecting the sun, he couldn't see how many people were inside, but no cars or trucks or sheriff's department SUVs followed. A good sign.

At least they had that much going for them.

He concentrated on breathing and composing his mind. He and Sarah would have time to work out whatever was bothering her. It would be fine. He had to believe that. Right now he had to focus on getting some answers from the reporter. And if he could win the guy's sympathies, all the better.

The car pulled in to the parking lot and a doughy-looking man wearing a blue polo shirt and khakis stepped out. He let himself in through the gate and walked around the trail, as Eric had instructed over the cell phone earlier.

Eric watched the car, but he detected no movement inside. From what he could tell, the reporter had indeed come alone.

Prohaska ambled down the trial with a shuffling, flat-footed gait. When he finally spotted Eric and Sarah, a smile played around the corners of his thin lips, not exactly happiness, but excitement. Chasing a story.

They made the introductions brief.

"Mind if I get this on tape?" the reporter asked.

"Go ahead." At least that way he'd have a record of what they knew…in case they were arrested, or killed before they could tell the story themselves.

"So how did it happen? How did you become a murderer?" Prohaska asked straight off.

"I didn't do it."

He screwed his lips to the side and shook his head as if disappointed. "All murderers say they didn't do it. Try walking into the state pen in Rawlins sometime. That's what they'll all tell you."

Eric shook his head. They didn't have time for this. "What do you know about Hodgeson?"

Prohaska's puffy smile faded. "I think he was murdered."

Eric nodded slowly, trying not to tip his hand, not until he learned more. "What makes you think that?"

"Like I said last night, I'm writing a book. I had one interview with the guy—kind of a dry one at that—and then he called me out of the blue." He paused, as if trying to lend dramatic import to his words.

"And said?" Sarah prodded.

Prohaska glanced from one to the other. "That he was planning to confess to a crime."

"A crime?" Sarah's eyes flew wide.

The wind was loud, swirling now. Maybe Eric hadn't heard him. He narrowed his eyes on the reporter. "What kind of crime?"

"Accepting bribes."

"From who?"

"You already know the who. You mentioned him last night. One of the biggest methamphetamine producers in the area. Walter Burne."

"So it was Burne's fingerprints in the meth lab?" Sarah asked. "And Hodgeson just lied?"

"Lied under oath. Add perjury to the list."

It didn't add up. Why take a bribe, lie on the witness stand and then confess for no reason? There had to be a reason. "Why would Hodgeson confess?"

"Because he was dying of emphysema. He was pretty far along. I guess he wanted to make sure his soul was prepared or something. I always wondered if I was jumping to conclusions about the murder, if he didn't decide to just kill himself instead."

Emphysema. Eric remembered an offhand comment Joy Hodgeson had made about her ex-husband being sick. And that he quit his job before his retirement benefits kicked in. But even though the circumstances seemed to suggest suicide, there was one detail that proved Hodgeson had been murdered more conclusively than the bullet hole in the back of his skull. "He didn't kill himself."

"You know that for a fact?"

"We found his body. Bullet hole in the skull."

"That doesn't rule out suicide."

"The place we found him does. At the base of Saddle Horn Ridge in the Absaroka Range. No way he could have gotten out there if he's in the later stages of emphysema."

The reporter nodded. "That sounds fairly solid."

"So Hodgeson threw Burne's case. Did he do that with any other cases?"

Prohaska shook his head. "Not that I could find. And I've looked, believe me. Ever since Hodgeson didn't show up at a meeting we were supposed to have, I've been trying to figure out what happened to him."

So he'd been working on the case for months and hadn't found anything. That didn't bode well for them.

Sarah tilted her head. "How about Danny Gillette? What can you tell us about him?"

"The Norris County Sheriff?" Prohaska's meaty brow creased. He lifted his shoulders in a jerky shrug. "Not much. Seems to do his job well, believes in America and apple pie and all that. Why do you ask?"

"So you don't know of any reason he has for wanting Larry Hodgeson dead?" Eric dropped the bombshell and watched for the reaction.

His eyes rounded. "You're saying Danny Gillette is responsible for killing Hodgeson?"

"And Randy Trask. And Glenn Freemont, too." added Sarah.

Prohaska lifted a hand, palm out. "Hold it right there. Can you prove any of this?"

A shot cracked through the canyon.

Eric's heart jumped to his throat. He stared at the reporter for a second as a red spot bloomed high on his shirt. Giving a low grunt, Prohaska flopped belly first into the dust.

Eric spun around, looking for where the bullet had come from. He hadn't seen anyone approach. Hadn't heard anyone.

Walter Burne stepped around the rock formation behind them, a handgun in his fist. "Hello, Sarah Trask. Where's my money?"

Eric's thoughts raced. This couldn't be happening. Where had Burne come from? How in the hell had he found them?

Sarah's eyes flared wide, her dark hair blowing in the wind. She glanced at Eric.

The drug dealer raised the gun and pointed the barrel straight at Sarah's face.

Pure, focused anger tightened Eric's muscles and hummed in his ears. Here he'd told Sarah that Burne wasn't a problem, nothing to worry about next to the sheriff. But he'd never expected this. How could he have been so wrong? He had to think. He had to stall. Scooping in a deep breath, Eric forced conviction past shaky lips. "Put the gun down. We have the money."

Burne lowered the gun a few inches, but still kept it pointed at Sarah. "You do, do you? Then give it to me. Now."

Eric had to do something. But what? He couldn't rush the scumbag. Burne wasn't standing that far away, but he could still get a shot off before Eric tackled him. A shot that would hurt Sarah...or kill her. He had to think of something else. Anything. And he needed to buy time until an idea came. "How did you find us?"

"I have my ways. I told you not to mess with me."

"The phone." Sarah's voice sounded choked. She wrapped her arms around her belly as if she could shield their baby from a bullet with flesh and bone.

"Very good. The lady wins a prize."

The phone. Of course. He knew police could find a cell phone by triangulating the signal between service towers. It had never occurred to him a guy like Burne could do the same, as long as he was willing to spread a little money around to the right people. Except for the time they'd spent waiting for Prohaska's call last night and the call to the reporter's cell phone today, he'd turned it off, for what good it had done. That last call had led Burne right to them.

Burne held out his hand, palm up. "Speaking of the phone, I'll take it back now."

Eric handed it over. If it wasn't their only link to the outside world, he'd be eager to be rid of the damn thing. "How did you know to come around the other side of the badlands? Why not just take the road?"

Burne gave him a look that said he'd seen through Eric's stalling tack. "Because I'm not an idiot. You have about two seconds to give me my money."

"It's on the ATV."

"Nice try, but I checked when I parked my bike next to it. Which makes me think you don't have the money at all. Do you?"

Eric's throat felt drier than the badlands themselves.

"I'm tired of this. It'll be worth twenty Ks just to watch the two of you die." He raised the gun. A crack split the air.

Sarah jolted and fell.

Chapter Seventeen

Eric threw himself at Burne, the gunshot ringing in his ears. He hit the man full force. The two of them flew backward. Eric landed on top of him on the craggy ground.

The drug dealer gasped for breath.

The scum had shot Sarah. He'd shot Sarah. Eric pulled back a fist and let it go, smashing into the man's face. His nose popped under the blow. Blood gushed through his nostrils. Eric pulled his fist back to hit him again.

Burne lurched upward, slamming his forehead smack into Eric's nose.

Eric reeled backward, stunned for a second, pain clanging through his head.

Burne bucked his body, shoving Eric back and to the side. He brought something up. Something he held with both fists.

The gun.

Eric lashed out with his hands. His first thought was to block the bullet from crashing into him. But once his hands were moving, they seemed to take on an intention of their own. A will that moved faster than thought. He grabbed the gun, the barrel hot against his fingers. He pulled, trying to wrest it from Burne's grip.

The scumbag's fingers clamped down on the weapon, his fists like iron. Strong for a weasel. But not as strong as Eric.

He grabbed Burne's wrist and twisted. Something popped. A grunt escaped Burne's clenched teeth. Still he didn't release the weapon.

Using all his strength, Eric twisted the gun around, still in the dealer's fist. He had shot Sarah. Eric would make him let go. He would make him pay.

The gun exploded between them.

At first, Eric wasn't sure what happened. Had the bullet gone wide? Had it hit him? He couldn't see anything but the man's shoulder. Couldn't feel anything but searing heat. Couldn't smell anything but burned gunpowder.

Then he smelled blood.

Burne gurgled deep in his throat. He stared at Eric with eyes that didn't see. Wetness oozed through a hole in the black leather duster. He shuddered and slumped to the ground. Limp fingers released the gun, leaving it in Eric's hands.

Dead? Hurt? Eric didn't know. Didn't care. All he could think about was getting back to Sarah. Making sure she was all right.

She *was* all right. She had to be.

He struggled to his feet and stumbled across the craggy ground, loose rock shifting under his feet. His heart thudded as if trying to break through his rib cage. She was lying fifteen feet from the reporter, crumpled in the place he'd seen her go down.

Please make her be alive. Please.

He fell to his knees beside her. She moved her head, meeting his eyes with a tight-lipped grimace.

Thank God.

"You're going to be okay. You're going to be okay." He didn't know if he kept repeating the words for her sake or his. Either way, he couldn't stop. "You're going to be okay."

A dark stain marred her jeans, the spot encompassing her whole thigh and growing. A tear marked the center of the indigo cotton.

"Burne?" Her voice was barely loud enough to hear over the wind.

"He's no longer a problem."

She nodded and asked nothing further.

"I'm going to look here. I'm going to see…"
He fitted his fingers into the edges of the hole
and pulled. The fabric gave, only a little, but it
was enough to see blood pulsing from the
puncture in her skin.

"How bad?"

"Not bad. It's going to be fine." A leg wound.
It could be worse. She wouldn't die from that.
Not, unless, she lost too much blood.

His throat felt tight. The thought of losing
Sarah, of losing their baby…he could hardly
breathe. He needed to think. He needed something to stop the bleeding. He fumbled with the
buttons on his shirt. His fingers were thick,
clumsy, trembling. Too big to fit buttons into
holes. Grabbing each side of the fabric, he
pulled, popping the buttons. He slipped the shirt
off his back and wadded it into a ball, then
pressed it against Sarah's leg. "I have to get
you to a hospital."

"Hospital? No."

"I can't handle this on my own."

"You said it was fine."

"It is. It will be. If you get to a hospital,
you'll be fine."

"But the sheriff…" A sob shook from her chest. "The sheriff. He'll find us."

She was right. The hospital would report a gunshot wound. The sheriff would find them.

He lifted the balled-up shirt from her thigh. Blood pulsed out of the wound, another wave seeping into her jeans. He clamped the cotton and fleece down tight. This couldn't be happening. He felt dizzy. Like he couldn't set his mind to reality. Like he was floating outside, somehow, watching events happening to other people. People he didn't know.

Sarah gritted her teeth. Her eyes looked shiny, glassy. The lines of her beautiful face contracted with pain. "A leg wound isn't going to kill me."

"It'll be…" He closed his mouth. Who was he trying to kid? It wasn't going to be fine. She wasn't going to be okay. Not unless he did something. Not unless he did something now.

Heat suffused his chest. Lose her. He could lose her. To blood loss. If not that, infection. Chaos spun through his mind, turning his stomach, making him want to double over in pain.

This was what had held him back four months ago. This. Not emotion or lack of control or anything else. If he never loved her, he would never lose her.

Problem was, he loved her with everything he was.

"I'm taking you to the hospital."

"Don't." She shook her head, several dark hairs sticking to the tears streaking down each cheek.

"There's no choice."

A groan came from behind him. Eric spun around.

The reporter moved his arm in the dust. Slowly, back and forth. He tried to lift his head but fell back against rock. He was alive.

With two people in need of medical care, two people he wasn't sure he could move, Eric knew he couldn't handle this on his own.

He grabbed Sarah's hand and pressed it to the shirt on her leg. The cotton was nearly saturated already and squished under her palm. "Hold this. Put as much pressure on it as you can stand."

She gritted her teeth and pressed down. "What are you going to do?"

"What I have to."

"Eric? What does that mean?"

He let out a long breath. Reaching out a hand, he brushed his fingers over her forehead, pushing back stray hair. "I've figured some things out, Sarah. About me. About what has been holding me back. I love you, Sarah. I love you, and I don't care if you believe it or not. And no matter what happens, I'm not going to let you die."

She made a small sound deep in her throat. A sigh, a whimper, he wasn't sure.

He leaned down and kissed her forehead. He'd been so stupid. He'd wasted so much time. Time he could have used making Sarah happy. Being happy himself. Time that could have meant something. Now he was nearly out.

He stood and stepped over the harsh terrain, making his way to where the meth dealer lay on his back. The man stared up into the wide Wyoming sky. Already his eyes looked opaque and dull, his complexion more like rubber than flesh.

Eric unzipped the man's coat. His whole chest was soaked with blood, making it impossible to tell the true color of the shirt underneath. He ran his hands over the man's pants and inside the coat. Finding what he was looking for in a pocket in the lining, he pulled it out with a sticky hand.

He knew water would ruin a cell phone. He hoped the same wasn't true for blood.

SARAH STRUGGLED TO raise her head, to see what Eric was doing. Nausea claimed her stomach. She lowered her head back to the rocky ground and focused on breathing. In and out. In and out. Eric's words ran through her mind, over and over again, like an old compact disc stuck on Repeat.

He loved her. He loved her.

She'd wanted so badly to hear those words. Months ago, before he'd left and nearly every day since. But now that he'd finally said them, what did they mean? What did they matter?

A chill penetrated her skin, deepening until it worked into her bones. Her leg had stopped hurting. Really since that first cold, cutting sensation, the pain hadn't been as bad. Not as bad as her bloody jeans would suggest it should be. And that had her scared more than anything.

She heard a rustling from nearby. The shuffle of footsteps over rocky soil.

Eric loomed over her, his face cloaked in shadow, blocking the sun. He took the wadded-up shirt from her hands. She could feel the pressure increase on her leg. "How are you doing?" he asked.

She shivered. "Cold."

He gripped her hand, rubbing it between his palms. "You're probably going into shock. Don't worry. Layton will be here soon."

"You called Layton?"

"I couldn't think of anyone who could do a better job of protecting you." He smiled, but his eyes didn't twinkle the way they did when he was teasing or wanted to kiss her or even the time she'd caught him watching her while she slept.

"What about you?"

He looked away, craning his neck to stare down the road as if willing Layton's truck to crest the hill.

"You're going to run, right?"

His chest rose and fell, sweat slicking his bare skin.

He didn't have to say it. She could tell from the weight of his silence that he'd made his decision. A decision he thought he had to make to protect her. "You can't be here when Layton arrives, Eric. He might bring the sheriff."

He pressed his lips into a bloodless line.

"Eric, the sheriff will kill you."

"Layton said he won't."

So he'd made a deal with Layton. If Layton took care of her, he'd turn himself in to the sheriff. She felt tired, so tired. As if getting each word out of her mouth was a desperate undertaking. "Please."

"I had to."

For her. He was doing this for her. Giving himself to the sheriff. Throwing his life away to make sure she was safe. "Eric." Her voice sounded dry in her throat, dryer than the land she was lying on.

He leaned close to her, his mouth only inches away, and suddenly all she could think about was kissing him. Pulling him down to her. Tasting his passion. Here she was hurt, Eric was going to die, and the only thing she could focus on was how much she wanted him. How much she needed him. And how she might never see him again. "I don't want to lose you, either, Eric."

Tears glistened in his eyes. "You have to trust me."

Trust him? Trust him to do what? Get himself killed? Throw his life away in exchange for hers? "You're not listening."

He leaned a little closer. "I'm listening now."

"Run."

He shook his head. "That won't work. They'll have you."

"But at least they won't have you, too."

"And when they threaten to hurt you, then what should I do, Sarah? Turn and walk away?"

"Yes. Pretend you don't care."

"And you think they'll believe that? You think they'll believe I would let you and our baby get hurt? Die? Because I'm not that good at pretending, Sarah."

A shiver shook her, one she would never be able to warm. "What did you tell Layton? What did you promise you'd do?"

"He's coming to take you to the hospital. The sheriff is with him. If I go without a fight, he'll say I kidnapped you. I made you go with me against your will. You won't be charged with anything. And you'll go to the hospital. They'll stop the bleeding. You'll be okay. Our baby will be okay."

So that was it. Just what she'd feared.

Tears streamed down her cheeks. Pain hollowed out her chest. Emptiness. She couldn't let Eric give his life, yet he was right about the baby. She had to think of their unborn child. "Layton will make sure I get to the hospital no matter what else happens. You don't have to make this bargain."

"Here he comes. Just hold on, Sarah. Everything is going to be okay. I promise."

Even without lifting her head, she could see the plume of dust rising from the road. "Eric."

"I'm not leaving you."

"Please, Eric."

He shook his head. "I told you I would never leave you, and I meant it. I love you, Sarah."

She'd yearned to believe those words. Prayed for it. Never thought she could really let herself. But she believed him now.

Only now it was too late.

Chapter Eighteen

The sheriff's white SUV followed Layton's pickup into the tiny parking area. Sarah watched it approach, her eye drawn to a black-and-white dot in the truck's bed just before the world smeared into a blurry mosaic of color.

She blinked back her tears but it was no good.

Layton climbed from the truck, a red box in his hand that Sarah identified as the first-aid kit he always kept in his truck for the horses and ranch hands. He ran along the trail, heading straight for them. The sheriff dismounted from his vehicle and followed in Layton's wake. As he drew closer, he pulled a gun from his holster and leveled it on Eric. "Stand back from her, son."

Eric gave her a long look, then slowly climbed to his feet and took several paces back.

The sheriff positioned himself between Eric and Sarah. He put his back to the edge of a small drop in the canyon. "That's fine. Stop right there."

Layton ducked to her side. He kneeled down and looked into her eyes. "Oh, Sarah." His voice ached with worry, with pain.

She had the urge to fold herself into his arms, to let him make things all better like he'd always tried to do when she was a kid and her parents had just had a knock-down-drag-out or Randy had just done something stupid and risky. "You can't let the sheriff take Eric, Layton. He'll kill him."

He lifted the saturated shirt from her thigh and replaced it with two layers of cotton quilting used under horses' leg wraps. "Ain't nothing I can do, honey."

She opened her mouth to correct him, to make him see, then closed it without speaking. It was no use. Layton had never believed Eric was innocent. He'd only gone along with it, because he'd been scared for her.

"Let me see your hands," the sheriff ordered.

Eric raised his hands, palms out. "Get Sarah to a hospital. Dennis Prohaska here, too. I think he's still alive."

The sheriff glanced down at the still bulk of the reporter, then back at Eric. "So you had to drag someone else into this mess?"

Eric raised his chin and met the sheriff's eyes straight on. "You'll find your boy Burne over there." He motioned to the other side of the rock formation with a nod of his head. "I hope he paid your bribe in full, because he's not going to be able to make good on any outstanding promises."

The sheriff frowned. He glanced at Layton. "Burne? Who the hell is Burne?"

"There's no reason to pretend." Sarah knew she should keep her mouth shut, but the words flowed out on a tide of anger and frustration, injustice and grief. "We know he paid you to kill Larry Hodgeson."

The sheriff swung his gaze to her. A chuckle broke from his lips. "Oh, you know that, do you? I guess you were right, Layton. We don't have to worry about this one."

Layton kept his eyes on Sarah's wound as if he hadn't heard the sheriff, even though they weren't that far apart. He wrapped a pressure bandage around her leg as tenderly as he could, securing the quilts over the wound.

"Hodgeson was paid, too, wasn't he, Sheriff?" Eric said. "Just like you. Paid to do whatever a drug dealer wanted. Even kill."

The sheriff shook his head. "Get down on the ground. On your belly."

"Get Sarah and Prohaska to the hospital. Then I'll do whatever you say, no fight. Just like we agreed."

"You won't fight me now. Not unless you want a bullet in your head."

"Some threat, Gillette. That's been your idea all along, hasn't it?"

The sheriff's shoulders seemed to slump, just a little, as if he was as bone tired as they were. "None of this has been my idea, son. Trust me on that."

None was his idea? Sarah wanted to scream. "Then why are you doing this? Money?"

The sheriff scoffed and shook his head. "I'm not for sale. Don't you forget it. I've never been for sale."

"Then why?" She didn't understand. Maybe she never would. He had men kill her brother. Same for Bracco and Glenn. Now he was going to kill Eric, and for what? "Why are you doing this?"

"Why?" He let out a long breath as if blowing smoke through tight lips. "Justice, that's why."

The most ridiculous answer Sarah had ever heard. "How does what you're doing have anything to do with justice?"

"We agreed. Sarah's out of this." Layton's voice rang vicious as a growl.

The sheriff shrugged a shoulder. "The lady asked."

Sarah looked from Layton to the sheriff. Something was going on between them. An argument unvoiced. "What does justice have to do with Randy's death? How about Glenn Freemont? And Eric? How can any of what you've done have to do with justice?"

Eric took a step forward.

The sheriff spun to face him. "On your belly, Lander. Now."

Eric didn't move.

Sheriff Gillette swung around and pointed the gun at Sarah.

Layton sucked in a breath. "Dan."

"Fine. Fine. I'm down." Eric lowered himself onto his stomach, hands and legs straight out from his body.

The sheriff swung his weapon back in Eric's direction. "Cross your ankles and place your hands behind your head."

This time, Eric followed instructions.

Tears clogged Sarah's throat. Her stomach swirled. Her leg started throbbing, making her wish with each beat of her pulse that she could go back to numbness. But no physical pain was as bad as what was unfolding in front of her. What she couldn't understand, let alone stop. "I don't think you know the meaning of the word *justice*."

The sheriff grimaced. He shook his head. "It wasn't supposed to happen this way. It was never supposed to happen this way."

"Then why are you doing it?"

The sheriff didn't look at her. Instead, he stared at the rock formation beyond the spot where Eric lay, as if he was talking to a ghost. Or just muttering to himself. "It's not the way things should work. He's guilty. He was sentenced. He needs to pay."

Guilty? Sentenced? What was he talking about? Burne had been acquitted. Unless he wasn't talking about Burne. Unless he was talking about someone else.

She thought of the articles Eric had read in the library. The other cases in which Hodgeson had testified, and the very important one where he'd delivered the crucial piece of evidence to get a conviction. "You're talking about the drunk driver who killed your sister."

The sheriff spun around and stared at her as if he'd just discovered she was still there. "How do you know about that?"

"Sarah." Eric's voice was muffled, his face down in the dust, but she could still hear the warning tone in his voice, clear as if he'd shouted.

He wanted her to keep quiet. To not put the pieces together, to not push for the truth. He wanted her to let things just go on as they were. Where the sheriff put a bullet in his brain to keep him quiet, and she walked away, with Layton at her side protecting her.

But the problem with that was, if what she thought was right, the sheriff couldn't let her walk away, either. He would have to kill them all. At least if they acted now, if she made Eric and Layton understand, their odds would be three to one.

She knew Eric would believe her. He might have already added up all the pieces on his own. But Layton? If they were going to get out of this, she needed to convince Layton.

"Hodgeson was going to give himself up, wasn't he, Sheriff? He was going to admit he took a bribe to lie about the fingerprints in the drug case against Walter Burne."

The sheriff glowered at her, but he didn't argue. He didn't say a word.

"The only problem with him confessing was that it would call all his fingerprint identifications into question, wouldn't it? All the finger-print evidence Hodgeson analyzed in crimes across the whole state."

Her hands shook. Her back was slick with clammy sweat, but she forced herself to continue. She focused on Layton and willed him to understand. "And that means the drunk driver who killed the sheriff's sister would get a new trial. That is, if the state decided to spend the money trying him again at all. If they didn't just let him go with time served."

Layton closed his eyes. His shoulders slumped forward. He looked tired. Old. His face gaunt and mouth slack. "Oh, God, Sarah."

She reached out and gripped his shoulder. "It's true, Layton. It all adds up. You've got to believe me."

"Oh, he believes you," the sheriff said.

"Layton?" She looked from Layton to the sheriff and back again. A weight settled, sick in her stomach. It hadn't dawned on her. The entire time she'd been outlining the sheriff's situa-tion, it hadn't dawned on her once.

The drunk who killed the sheriff's sister had been convicted on the strength of fingerprint evidence. It had happened only eight years ago. Recent enough to be in the newspaper's Internet archives.

But he wasn't the only one who'd had a loved one murdered.

A murder solved by fingerprint evidence. A murder that could be tried anew or even overturned. Sheriff Danny Gillette wasn't the only one here willing to do anything to preserve justice.

She looked up at her mentor, her father in heart and word and deed. But he was the real father of another girl before he even knew her. A girl who was taken from him. A girl for whom he'd pledged his life to see justice was done.

And that it stayed done. "Layton, how could you have murdered my brother?"

EVEN FROM TWENTY feet away, lying facedown in the dirt, Eric could see Layton's face blanch. The older man opened his mouth, then shut it without saying a word. Tears wound down his worn cheeks.

"Your brother was a troublemaker, Ms. Trask. Always was," the sheriff said. Even he sounded tired, beaten down like Layton. "He was a loser out for an easy buck, whether he had to cheat, steal or cook drugs to get it."

Sarah raised her chin. Her eyes hardened. The

breeze blew back her hair. "He didn't deserve to die." She looked like a warrior woman protecting her own. Breathtaking. Beautiful.

And if Eric had anything to say about it, she wasn't going to fight this war alone.

Slowly he moved his hands off the back of his head. He uncrossed his ankles. With Sarah commanding the sheriff's and Layton's attention, maybe he could get into a better position unseen, a position where he could attack the lawman and take his gun.

The sheriff tilted his hat back and wiped a hand across his forehead. "If you want to blame someone, blame Randy himself. He was the one who went looking for Hodgeson's body for his own gain. Or blame Hodgeson. He's the one who took the drug dealer's bribe. And then he had to ease his conscience, damn the consequences. Damn the whole system."

"They didn't kill anyone," she said.

"Really? Both of them would have brought down the whole justice system if we'd let them. You think flooding the courts with appeals for new trials isn't going to lead to some criminals being set free? Criminals who should rightly spend eternity behind bars? Criminals who will take more innocent lives as a result?"

She looked from the sheriff to Layton. "You took Randy's life."

The sheriff was the one who answered. "Your brother went looking for Hodgeson's body so he could blackmail us."

"I don't believe you," Sarah stammered.

"Believe it," the sheriff said. "He paid me a visit as soon as he was released from jail."

Sarah was silent for a long time. Finally she spoke. "How about Glenn? He was an innocent."

"Glenn Freemont? An innocent?" The sheriff barked out a smoker's laugh. "Not hardly. He was a coward with a weak stomach. He couldn't stick to the plan. He talked big about justice, but when it came to doing what was required, he couldn't hack it."

"Glenn? He was working with you?"

The sheriff didn't answer, but he didn't have to.

Eric tensed his arms, ready to raise himself in a push-up and from there, spring to his feet. He had to move slowly, carefully. One sound or sense of movement and it would be over.

"And Keith Sherwood? Is he working for you, too?"

"Keith Sherwood? He's a loser. Has an obsession with guns and no sense of responsibility to go with it. A loose cannon and a drunk, that's what he is. Do you think I'd take a chance on someone like that?"

Eric took his weight onto his arms and gathered his legs under him. So they'd been wrong about Keith Sherwood. It had been Glenn Freemont and Layton who had dressed as deputies and shot Randy.

"And this Bracco who died in jail. That wasn't suicide, was it? You killed him, too."

The sheriff continued. "You have no idea what a piece of scum Bracco was. If you want another one to blame, he's a good one. Him and his blabbing mouth. If he hadn't told Randy where to find Hodgeson's body, Randy wouldn't have been involved at all. I never should have trusted Bracco to help me take care of Hodgeson."

Sarah breathed hard, as if she couldn't quite catch her breath.

"We didn't mean to have any of this happen, Sarah." Layton's voice was so weak, Eric could barely hear it over the whistling wind. "We just couldn't…I couldn't let Allison's murderer get a new trial for something that had nothing to do with his case. Not when I could stop it. I couldn't risk that he'd go free on some technicality when he took my Allison away forever."

Sarah's face drew tight. "You killed Randy!"

"The blackmail... I couldn't risk... It couldn't be helped."

"And Eric?"

Eric held his breath, hoping Sarah's mention of his name wouldn't cause Layton to glance in his direction.

Sarah swiped at her eyes with the back of one hand. She paused, her gaze landing on him for a split second, then she focused back on Layton. "You and Glenn dressed as deputies and shot at them. You killed Randy in cold blood."

"I'm sorry, Sarah."

"And me? Were you going to kill me?"

She was provoking now, giving him a chance to get in position, to make his move. But even though Eric was grateful for the chance, deep down he wished she would stop. He didn't like the way she was challenging them, making herself a threat.

He couldn't lose her.

"I know too much now, don't I? You're going to have to kill me."

Layton shook his head. "No, I'll always protect you, Sarah. You know that. I'll never hurt you."

"It's necessary, Layton."

Layton twisted around and stared a hole

through the sheriff. "You gave me your word. If I brought you out here, you'd let me take Sarah to the hospital."

"That was before she added the whole thing up. Do you really think she is going to keep our secret? You shot her brother. We're about to shoot her lover. You really think she's as loyal to you as you are to her?" He swung the gun, pointing the barrel at Sarah.

Eric's breath froze in his chest. He crouched, hands and feet under him like a runner at the starting blocks, ready to charge, but he was too far away. The sheriff could pull the trigger, he could kill Sarah before Eric could reach him. He gasped in a breath, ready to shout, to focus the sheriff's gun back on him.

A growl ripped from the edge of the canyon.

The sheriff turned toward the sound.

A black-and-white form crouched among crags of tan and red rock. Radar had jumped out of the truck bed, as if he'd sensed the threat to his mistress.

The sheriff leveled his gun on the dog.

Eric leaped forward. Head down like a football player, he ran for all he was worth. He smacked into the sheriff just as the gun went off.

Chapter Nineteen

A scream broke from Sarah's throat. She struggled to get up, to run to Eric and Radar, to help. Pain stabbed through her leg and it refused to move.

Straddling the sheriff, Eric slammed a fist into the man's face. Again. Again.

Another shot cracked through the air, shaking through Sarah's body, ringing in her ears.

Eric grabbed the hand with the gun and pounded it against the ground. The weapon skittered across red rock and slipped into a dip in the canyon. Another punch, and the sheriff's head lolled back against the ground, his face red with blood.

Still on top of him, Eric fumbled with the sheriff's belt. Handcuffs jingled, mixing with the constant howl of the wind.

Another jingle came from the canyon's edge.

Radar rose from his crouch and slunk up through crags of rock. Head low, he wiggled to Eric's side. Submissive and afraid of the loud gunfire, but perfectly fine.

A breath shuddered through Sarah's chest. Eric. Radar. She focused on Layton, on the gun in the holster by his side.

He stared at Eric, watching him handcuff the sheriff as if in a trance. His jowls hung slack, his bushy brows sheltered low over moist eyes. His body slumped as if he was more than tired, as if he'd given up. A man beaten down by life.

She still couldn't wrap her mind around what he'd done. In her heart, she wanted him to always be the man she looked up to, relied on. But he wasn't that man. He was her brother's murderer.

Not only that, he'd shot at Eric before, tried to kill him. And he could do it again.

She reached for Layton's handgun. She didn't expect to get it so easily, and the roughness of the grip as her fingers closed around it came as a shock. She pulled it free of the holster. Fitting it into her palms, she slipped a finger into the trigger guard and pointed it at Layton. "It's all over."

He nodded but didn't look at her. Instead he focused on the dusty rock in front of him. "I'm sorry, Sarah. I'm so sorry."

"That's not enough."

"I know. When you lose someone you love, it's never enough. Allison's murderer was tried. He was locked away. Knowing he's locked away was the only thing I had to cling to. I couldn't risk that. But nothing makes up for what he's done."

No, she supposed it didn't. No matter what happened to Layton, Randy would never come back.

"Give me the gun, Sarah."

She narrowed his eyes. What, did he think she was out of her mind? "Not a chance."

"I'm not going to hurt you. Lander, either. But I don't want this to go on. I don't want you to suffer through a trial. And the fingerprints Hodgeson analyzed…it's all going to be called into question now, even the legitimate matches, even Allison's case. I don't want to see Allison's killer get another chance. Let me do the right thing. Let me save all of us a lot of pain."

He was talking about killing himself, and for a second, she thought about handing over the gun and letting him do it. The second passed. She shook her head. "I can't do that, Layton."

"It's the only thing that will make up for what I've done, Sarah. A life for a life. I would let you shoot me, but I know you'd never pull the trigger. So let me do it. Let me make things right."

"No, Layton. Things aren't that easy." A shadow fell over her. She looked up to see Eric eclipsing the sun. In his hands dangled a second set of handcuffs. Her eyes misted as he pulled Layton's hands behind his back and slipped the cuffs on his wrists. Eric pulled off Layton's boots next and secured his ankles just as he'd done to the sheriff.

She felt a nudge against her uninjured thigh. Glancing down, she watched Radar snuggle his nose into her, his tail wagging so hard his whole body vibrated.

She stroked her fingers over his black-and-white head. Her leg throbbed. The muscles in her back ached. But worst of all was the pain in her heart. Closing her eyes, she let the tears roll down her cheeks. It was amazing she could still cry, that she still had tears left, but she did. For Randy and Layton, for Glenn and the sheriff, for justice itself.

"It looks like the bleeding has slowed."

She opened her eyes to see Eric leaning over her, checking the bandage on her leg. His chest was covered in dust, his face bloody. But here he was, alive. "A miracle."

"A miracle." Eric nodded. Shadows cupped around his eyes. "I used Burne's cell to call 911. Deputies should be here soon."

Sarah's stomach tightened. She couldn't quite trust it was all over. The whole thing seemed unreal. "Will they believe us?"

"They'll have to. Prohaska has the whole thing on tape. The wind might have drowned out a few things, but most of it near the end is clear as a bell."

The reporter. She'd all but forgotten about him. "How is Prohaska?"

"In pain, but alive. The bullet hit him in the shoulder. A few inches lower, and he'd be gone."

Another miracle. "Can he talk?"

Eric chuckled, low in his throat. "Well enough to tell me he has a bestseller on his hands."

Sarah couldn't help but smile at that, even though none of what had happened was remotely happy. Relieved. That's what she was. Tired and relieved. She'd come close as a whisper to losing everyone she loved, but she hadn't…she hadn't. Eric and Radar, they were okay. They were here. And no matter what had happened—with Randy, with Layton—she knew she had the strength to go on.

But there was one last thing. Before the

deputies got there, before the EMS took her away, she needed to say something. She only hoped she could find the words. "Eric?"

He folded her hand in two of his. His touch was rough and warm and everything she needed. And for a moment she just sat there and soaked it in. And when she opened her mouth, the words were there, pouring out like a waterfall, clear and clean and sincere. "I believe in you, Eric. I believe in us. And from here on out, I always will."

His eyes took on a sheen that burrowed into her heart. "Does this mean you'll marry me?"

She nodded, warmth flooding through her. A giggle built in her throat and bubbled through her bloodstream, as intoxicating as champagne. She looked down at her leg. Red soaked through the pads and stained the pressure wrap. But none of it mattered. She'd live. She'd heal. And she and Eric had their second chance. "I'd love to marry you, Eric. As soon as I can walk down the aisle."

"Aisle? I was thinking we could say our vows in that little basin at the Buckrail, with the mountains as our church."

He remembered. Her stupid, offhand comment. Her childish dream. The thing she thought had destroyed their chances forever, and now it would cement their bond. "I'd like that. I'd like that a lot."

He moved close behind her. Careful not to disturb Radar or touch her injured thigh, he slipped a leg out on either side. She leaned back against his chest as if he was her easy chair. Her support. The muscles in her back eased, and for the first time in days, she let herself relax, just a little.

"I love you, Sarah." His voice tickled her ear and vibrated through her rib cage. "I want to hold you every day for the rest of my life. Not because I have to. Because I want to. More than anything."

He rested a gentle hand on her belly. And at that moment, she felt filled to the brim.

Epilogue

Eric hated being the bearer of bad news. Especially on a day like today. Sure, the air held a chill and the ground was dusted with enough snow that it really seemed winter had taken ahold of the Buckrail Ranch. But judging by a warm sun and cloudless sky that stretched on forever, neither of those things would hang into the afternoon.

Of course, weather wasn't the most glorious thing about this day.

He took a deep breath of the sweet scent of hay. The sound of grinding teeth hummed through the barn, comfortable, cozy, his morning chores already done.

Sarah would be awake soon. Sarah and Cody.

And that's what made today so special. It was the first day he, his wife and their sweet newborn son would enjoy breakfast together in their home.

If only he didn't have to ruin it.

He closed the barn door behind him and stepped out into the cold. A pickup rolled up the drive, gravel popping under tires. Eric tipped his hat to Keith at the wheel and the new hand, Steve, in the seat beside him, just arriving to start the day's work.

Eric had hated to quit the guide service at the beginning of the tourist season, but he hadn't had much choice. Getting through the summer and the fall roundup with only him, Keith and Steve had been rough, especially with Sarah laid up with her leg injury and her due date drawing near. But they'd made it.

As it turned out, Eric couldn't have done it without Keith. The kid had really cleaned up his act. Giving up booze had been tough for him, but it had really transformed his temperament and improved his work ethic. He and the new guy had more than pulled their weight. Selling off more cattle than usual had been a good move, too. And with the addition of guest cabins built over the summer, the Buckrail's transformation into a guest ranch would be complete by the time the next summer rolled around.

Eric would be back guiding tourists through

the wilderness, and giving them a wild west style ranching experience at the same time.

Perfect.

And by the time that happened, he hoped much of the hurt Sarah had been through in the past months would be over. Or at least faded.

He passed the corral and stepped up onto the porch. For a second, he paused, hand on doorknob, but then forced himself to push the door open and step inside.

The house smelled like fried eggs and toast, and his stomach growled despite the fact that he didn't feel at all hungry. He shrugged off his coat and boots. Best to tell her right away and get it over with. He'd already held the news back for one day, not wanting to spoil the baby's homecoming. She wouldn't forgive him if he held it back any longer.

Radar trotted into the foyer, toenails clicking on the hardwood floor. Mouth open and tongue peeking out between lower canines, he looked like he was smiling. No doubt he was. He'd added another human to his pack last night, and all evening, he hadn't wanted to stop licking the baby's head.

"Radar, where's Cody?"

The dog tilted his head from one side to the

other, as if trying his darnedest to decipher Eric's words. Turning, he trotted into the kitchen, as if he'd figured it all out.

Knowing Radar, he probably had.

Eric followed, his stocking feet whispering against the floor. When he reached the kitchen, Sarah was bent at the waist, hovering over the baby seat shaped a little like a bucket that sat on the table. Her hair draped around her face like a curtain. And in that curtain was tangled a pudgy little fist.

A chuckle bubbled from Eric's chest. "Good grip, huh?"

Sarah smiled up at him through her drape of hair. "I think he's going to be a roper. There's a lot of skill in these hands already. I can tell."

"Nah, he'll be climbing mountains by the time he's three."

Sarah laughed. "Maybe he'll do both."

Eric leaned down and kissed the soft fuzz on the newborn's head, then kissed Sarah. Warmth filled his chest as if the bright morning sun was shining from inside. He was so lucky. Sarah for his wife. A healthy baby boy. A future that was so bright it glowed. They just had to put away the past.

"What is it?" Having freed the baby's fingers

from her hair, Sarah narrowed her eyes on Eric. "Something's bothering you."

This was it. He had to tell her. He took a deep breath. "I got a call from the interim sheriff yesterday, before I picked you up at the hospital."

"And?"

"They found evidence that Randy was in Las Vegas around the time Burne gave him that money."

"So he gambled it away."

He nodded. "Probably thought he could pocket his winnings and still have the twenty thousand."

"Do they know what he was going to do with that money? Why Burne gave it to him in the first place?"

That was the question he'd been dreading. The truth they'd guessed at but hadn't wanted to face. The reason he'd wished he'd never gotten that call yesterday. "Yes, they know."

Sarah pressed her lips into a solid line and raised her chin. "What?"

Eric took a deep breath and pushed the words out. "He was setting up a meth lab for Burne."

Sarah's expression didn't change, but Eric could detect a slight droop to her posture, a slight sheen in her eyes. Her brother had let her down. Again. "I can't believe I didn't know about it. Setting up a meth lab, a gambling trip and trying to get the money back with a blackmail scheme. He lied about everything."

Eric took Sarah in his arms. He didn't know what to say. No words could make any of it better. All he could do was hold her and love her and keep working toward a future. Building their business. Building their family. And enjoying their love.

Sarah gave him a kiss and stepped back, wiping her eyes. "So does this mean it's over? Finally? Or is someone else going to show up wanting money?"

"That's the good news." He let a smile break over his lips, more an expression of relief than happiness. But he'd come to appreciate relief in recent months.

"What good news?"

"There was big crackdown on Burne's organization. A state methamphetamine task force rounded up a bunch of producers and dealers with ties to Burne. The sheriff said we should have nothing more to worry about."

"Is he sure?"

"I asked the same thing."

"And?"

"He said to rest easy."

"And other scams? Was Randy into anything else we should know about?"

"According to the sheriff, they've turned his life upside down and that's all they've found that we don't already know."

"Good." She moved to the stove and lifted the lid off the sauté pan. A heavenly scent of eggs, ham, cheese and vegetables filled the kitchen. She folded the omelet onto a plate and handed it to Eric. "I got some news this morning, too."

Eric carried his plate to the table and sat down next to his son who was now starting to doze. He wasn't sure he could take any more news today. He'd like to ignore it all and just concentrate on his wife and son and how happy they made him.

But of course, that wasn't the way the world worked. "Good news, I hope."

"Sheriff Gillette confessed."

Eric looked up from his plate, his first forkful in mid air. "To all of it?"

"He's admitting to shooting Hodgeson and paying Bracco to dispose of the body. He's admitting to killing Glenn. And he's admitting to conspiring with Layton and Glenn to kill Randy and try to kill you. And me."

It all seemed so long ago now, even though it wasn't even half a year. Still, in that time so much had changed. Layton had pleaded guilty to Randy's murder immediately and was already sentenced. He'd apologized to Sarah in the courtroom, his only defense being Hodgeson's accepting a bribe in the Burne case would taint all of his other cases, even the legitimate ones, and that his daughter's killer would get a new trial.

Unfortunately, Layton had been right about that. The courts were flooded with petitions for new trials. And among the petitions scheduled to be heard were the drunk driver who'd killed the sheriff's sister and the slumber party killer, both convicted nearly solely on fingerprint evidence.

He dropped his fork and pushed up from his chair. He crossed the floor and took Sarah into a giant hug. She was soft and warm and smelled of eggs and shampoo and baby, and he pulled in a deep breath.

Life wasn't perfect. It never would be. Tragedies would happen. Injustices. Loss. But as long as he had these moments—moments spent with his wife and son, moments of joy like he'd never known—he knew he could get through.

He knew every day would be a glorious adventure and love would flow like a virgin waterfall swollen by the melt of spring.

* * * * *

*Harlequin Intrigue top author
Delores Fossen presents
a brand-new series of
breathtaking romantic suspense!*
TEXAS MATERNITY: HOSTAGES
*The first installment available May 2010:
THE BABY'S GUARDIAN*

Shaw cursed and hooked his arm around Sabrina.

Despite the urgency that the deadly gunfire created, he tried to be careful with her, and he took the brunt of the fall when he pulled her to the ground. His shoulder hit hard, but he held on tight to his gun so that it wouldn't be jarred from his hand.

Shaw didn't stop there. He crawled over Sabrina, sheltering her pregnant belly with his body, and he came up ready to return fire.

This was obviously a situation he'd wanted to avoid at all cost. He didn't want his baby in the middle of a fight with these armed fugitives, but when they fired that shot, they'd left him no choice. Now, the trick was to get Sabrina safely out of there.

"Get down," someone on the SWAT team yelled from the roof of the adjacent building.

Shaw did. He dropped lower, covering Sabrina as best he could.

There was another shot, but this one came from a rifleman on the SWAT team. Shaw didn't look up, but he heard the sound of glass being blown apart.

The shots continued, all coming from his men, which meant it might be time to try to get Sabrina to better cover. Shaw glanced at the front of the building.

So that Sabrina's pregnant belly wouldn't be smashed against the ground, Shaw eased off her and moved her to a sitting position so that her back was against the brick wall. They were close. Too close. And face-to-face.

He found himself staring right into those sea-green eyes.

How will Shaw get Sabrina out?
Follow the daring rescue
and the heartbreaking aftermath in
THE BABY'S GUARDIAN
by Delores Fossen,
available May 2010 from Harlequin Intrigue.

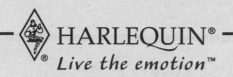

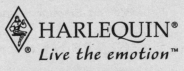

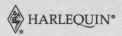

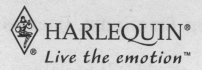

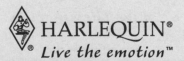

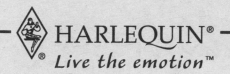